For my family

Busy

Sometimes optimism just isn't enough.

* * *

Jill across the road has started power-walking. At least, I think she has. She was belting along in a baseball cap and hoodie this morning as I was coming back from school. She waved because she is a nice person. I have had to revise my initial impression of her, formed when she was standing outside the supermarket with a couple of older women. They were talking to each other while she waited with her mouth slightly open, looking vacant. I felt superior because I was doing my shopping unaccompanied and with my mouth shut. Subsequently it has come to my attention that Jill is tall with a stunning figure, a permanent natural tan, the smartest house in the avenue and an easy relationship with her children, who are all the same ages as mine. Plus she is seven years younger than me.

*

I need new glasses. The hard little teardrops that rest on my nose have started to leave red welts. This was pointed out to me by the children's dentist. In a pretence of aghast surprise, I removed the glasses and looked at them. Why? It was then inescapably obvious to us both that they were extremely scratched and greasy.

When I put on this weight, seemingly even my nose expanded.

*

I couldn't wear a baseball cap, partly because of the glasses and partly because of my profile, which – as I recently discovered via my first experience of a changing room with a three-sided mirror – is really quite ugly. It turns out I have a nose like a beak, an upper jaw several sizes bigger than the lower and a receding chin. None of this is apparent, head-on. If I wore a baseball cap, I'd look like Jonathan King, which is not a good look for a woman.

*

Could much adolescent unhappiness have been avoided had I known what I really looked like? Did I behave as though I were pretty when I was not, and did people hate me for it? I didn't know.
I didn't know.

*

'Greet the unseen with a cheer!' This is one of my Uplifting Quotes, but I can't remember who said it (although probably not the Earl of Gloucester). The more I don't know, the more I want to, as I must find out whether it was a person who faced great suffering or really none at all.

*

Top of the Urgent list this morning was cleaning the toilets and bathroom, and now they gleam, but everywhere else is mess and gloom. My incompetence as a housekeeper seems to have increased, if anything, since the children were babies. How can this be, now that I have all the morning when they are at school? How can it take me half a day to clean a bathroom and two toilets? There are women surgeons, no doubt, who have whipped through such tasks before attending to a morning theatre list of tumours and bullet wounds.

*

I would like to see the look on his face if the surgeon doing his precious vasectomy turns out to be a woman.

*

I haven't really been comfortable using the word 'toilet' for a toilet since I discovered the classier 'lavatory' alternative. So, now I wish I had been brought up in a family who used 'lavatory' as standard, because it's far too late for me to switch, detesting, as I do, affectation (in myself; sometimes I can quite like it in others).

11

As if that were the regret worth singling out about my family.

'Detesting, as I do, affectation'? Like, that's not affected. The blinking has come back.

* * *

When you have pushed out a large turd on to the delivery table, before the watching eyes of two midwives, an anaesthetist and him, you think, Embarrassment is dead to me, now. Wrong. This morning at the roundabout a girl who looked like Joey Ramone was trying to cross the road with her baby in a buggy. She was dressed for a spring morning – which was optimistic, though it is spring – and it was starting to rain. He just drove on like she wasn't there. I squirmed beside him, but she grinned. Why?

He always sees racing-green BMWs nosing out at junctions, and then it's all gentlemanly standing aside, Come ahead, my good friend, come ahead. But he never sees women trying to cross the road with toddlers by the hand, and he never sees old people with nylon shopping bags and perforated shoes quivering on the kerb. At such moments, I cannot see the point of him.

And *he* is the one who presumes to lecture *me* about two generations of war heroes and poppies and minutes' silence for the fallen! Just so long as the survivors aren't getting in his way sixty years later, trying to cross the road back to their nursing homes.

*

He is going out with Woods tonight. I like it when he's out. I can do things my way and be tucked up in bed by nine. Bliss. (Nobody says 'Bliss' any more. Is this simply because the expression is *passé*, or have we lost all capacity for contentment?)

I don't like the part when he comes in with the bitter juice steaming out of his pores. He'll be sick, which he does very tidily, but he'll still smell contagious when he shambles into bed, and I'll disinfect the toilet and basin in the morning.

*

I think the blinking is connected to tiredness. I think it's just something I do when I'm tired.

* * *

Stephanie next door has got a vibrator. It took me a while to work out what it was. I was in bed, pillowed up against the party wall with my book, when I heard the high little strimmer sound. At first, I couldn't identify it, never actually having held or heard a vibrator in real life, but I'm not completely naïve: a couple of minutes' whirring in the bedroom, then a little pause, then they turn on the radio? It wasn't a hand-held blender.

This is yet another example of my double standards. The couple next door indulges in use of a vibrator, and I think: Racy. If it were us, I would be thinking: Desperate. Probably because Stephanie is blonde with long legs and Pete is a body builder, while we are just Us.

*

His big night out failed to materialise. Woods went off with a female member of the bar staff, and he was left alone and came home early – still radiating alcohol fumes but at least no actual disinfectant necessary.

*

There are certain spoken words over which it is only polite to stumble slightly. 'Reciprocity' is one. Anyone who can hurtle unimpeded through a sentence in which they decide at some point to use the word 'reciprocity' is lacking a sense of the human connection (givers of Royal Society Christmas Lectures excepted). It is perfectly acceptable and understood that people are fluent on 'reciprocal', but use of 'reciprocity' needs a certain hesitance and a slight smile, to acknowledge that the speaker is now grasping for the less familiar derivation with its unexpected footwork. Failure to acknowledge this looks a bit like showing off, and nobody likes a show-off.

Actually, everybody loves a show-off. Look at Elvis. Look at Jesus! Ah, but: Jesus wasn't merely a show-off, but also 'a man of sorrows and acquainted with grief'. Aren't we all?

Except for people who don't hesitate over 'reciprocity', obviously.

*

Jesus also invented the capsule wardrobe, by the way. 'One robe on and one in the wash', I think he said. In his part of the world, this meant one robe, full stop. Because you could wash it before you went to bed, hang it on the line, and it would be dry in the morning. I know this because I have done it (shorts and a T-shirt, in my case). I didn't have a spiritual awakening in the Holy Land, because I was too young. Here is how young I was. Once when we went hunting for casual work near the Egyptian border, we found a private beach enclosed by a ten-foot fence. There was a full-height turnstile where we peeked through and saw tables with parasols, but the place was deserted. I was *so* thin and *so* stupid (i.e., very, *very* young), I squeezed through the padlocked turnstile. I couldn't find anybody to ask for a job. What if there had been guard dogs (like the ones in the warning pictures!)? Or men with guns? What if I had got stuck in the turnstile and died of thirst? But I didn't see such possible outcomes until I was years and years and continents away.

Remember the smell of Jerusalem, of the Arab quarter. Warm, damp, overripe fruit and bread, ancient stone and undertones of urine. Little children played a game round an old sofa on the Via Dolorosa.

*

Is it normal, under any circumstances, to live in dread of your undealt-with post? I have one cardboard box, two long-life carrier bags and a kitchen drawer full of envelopes, and they keep me in perpetual torment. It's not even all mine to neglect. When the previous elderly householder died in a care home, his son telephoned to request in a humble yet charming way that I send on any of his deceased father's mail that might mistakenly persist in coming to our address. This is just the kind of help I love to be asked for because it is so easy to be generous. It's like when strangers approach you for directions and then think you're saintly because you *lead* them to their destination instead of merely *advising* them. This postal favour was so modest and untaxing that I proudly anticipated supplementing it with a chatty note about the house's new life, ringing with the sound of happy, playing children, or perhaps a charity donation in lieu of flowers as per the bereaved family's notice in the newspaper. So why, eighteen months later, do I have a heap of correspondence so huge and so heavy that I cannot forward it by ordinary mail (it wouldn't fit through a letterbox) yet cannot send by parcel post because it is unbearable to cost a working man his evening retrieving a mysterious package from the sorting office, knowing as I do that it is mainly full of last year's seed catalogues?

*

When is the last time a stranger asked me for directions? When I lived in cities, people often did. Perhaps then I looked more approachable. But, really, I know it is also because we do not get visitors, in these parts.

*

In these parts? Who am I, Joe Grundy?

*

Right. I am going to chip away. I am going to deal with five items of postal backlog each day, plus I am going to process today's mail today, every day. I am going to stop feeling defeated and guilty and become a woman of action.

*

With my immense postal backlog and associated feelings of failure, it is surely perverse that I am disappointed on days like today when nothing comes in the post.

* * *

This morning, I have filed an old oil bill and an electricity bill-type acknowledgement; I have binned an order form for new school jumpers, which should have been returned three months ago; and I have written hospital clinic appointments and dates for the parent teacher meetings into the Family Organiser. Five items of postal backlog, gone! Hooray!

*

A particularly pedantic English-speaker might point to the double-negative in *'Je ne regrette rien'* and assert that Edith Piaf was sorry about her whole bloody life.

* * *

Trevor is running for election. (Trevor is Jill's husband. His family owns the kind of old-fashioned shoe shop that specialises in leather brogues and zip-up slippers. We buy the black school shoes there.) He is standing for the Salt-of-the-Earth-God-Helps-Those-Who-Help-Themselves Party, which might mean an end to his football weekends away with the lads as I'm not sure the party fathers encourage that kind of thing. Jill and the children are having a studio portrait done with him on Monday for the campaign leaflets.

Had another look at the baseball-cap situation, with the help of the shaving mirror alongside the dressing table. Still Jonathan King. Not as bad without the glasses, but the beak-type peak seems to emphasise the beak-type nose, so still no.

*

There are two kinds of people who are very good at knowing what other people want and giving it to them. People like me (needy) and people like Woods (charmer). People like me are really tuned into what others want to hear. We watch and we listen, we identify it in a minute and we hand it straight over. People like Woods identify it just as quickly, but they get a glint in their eye, and they say, 'I know you, I know all about you, I know what you want, and, because I like you, I'm going to give it to you. But only because I like you.' That's the difference. And I don't know what it means.

*

I saw the girl who looks like Joey Ramone again this morning, in the post office. She is a brave girl, looking like Joey Ramone in a town like this where the dress code is: don't wear anything people can describe.

Often the word 'indescribable' is used when what is actually meant is 'describable' (eminently describable, even, using colour-words and size-words and words like 'noisy', 'daring' and 'spiky'). Try describing invisible. *I* am indescribable.

*

A totally wasted weekend. Hell is other people? *Mais non, Monsieur Sartre.* Hell is other people's children. *Les enfants terribles des autres.* Let's not go into it, but I like mine a lot better, right now.

*

OK. Greeting the unseen with a cheer, now, and there's rather a lot of unseen at present, as the legs of my glasses appear to have become baggy, if that is possible. Every time I lean forward, they fall off. They have already fallen into my dinner, and they depart every time I look down to brush the kitchen floor, which I cannot see sufficiently well to brush without them. This is where having no money becomes seriously irritating.

*

If God is Love, then why not just say Love?

*

And if Love is Blind, what does that make God?

*

I think there may be an actual, factual reason for my debilitating sense of inadequacy around other adults. Since I stopped working (for money) and had the children, I have suspended my human development. I have completely skipped *group dynamics* and *interpersonal skills* alongside all rites of passage involving colleagues' miscarriages, suicidal teenagers and Alzheimer's-ridden parents. I haven't learned through other people's experiences because there are no other people. I am frozen at the age of twenty-six, while the paperwork says I am so, so much older.

*

Every time my glasses fall off, I mutter, '*Fuck*,' while every time I inadvertently hurt myself, I mutter, '*Shit*.' I think I must use 'fuck' for sudden, unexpected but not completely unforeseeable misfortunes, because I would also say it if, for example, I ran out of cheques or went somewhere without first establishing the opening hours and found it closed. However, I seem to use 'shit' when something painful happens without any warning that is obvious to me. I don't use these terms showily, like an adolescent, but I do utter them. In fact, I utter them loudest when there is no one but me to hear them and most discreetly when innocent bystanders are within earshot. (Just once, I would like to hear of a *guilty* bystander – and make it a *heinously culpable* one at that.)

This evening, having made the mistake of trying to cross on foot three lanes of busy traffic (something I would never do with the children), I wondered how I would respond were I to miscalculate and be struck by the next car coming from my right. I recognised then that in that blinding second of rubber and asphalt and blood and steel, I would not gasp, scream or be flung in silence. Rather, as my brain first acknowledged the impact, I would certainly grunt, 'Shit', or 'Fuck', but which? (My sarcastic heart would be sneering: 'Greet that, bitch.')

*

I haven't seen Jill out power-walking again. Is this because she lacks will-power, and has quit, or because she has found a friend with whom to power-walk in another part of town? Perhaps she has joined Dancercise classes at the leisure centre, or has discovered a sexier option, like swimming or salsa. I am disgusted to find that I want the explanation to be lack of will-power, despite the cost to Jill's health and associated risk to her longevity as mother to three young children.

*

We have been leafleted by Trevor's lot, who are quickest off the mark. They already have Trevor's picture up on lamp-posts all over town. How can he stick it? I cringe when the chemist's assistant flashes one of my holiday snaps to ensure she is giving me the correct packet. Even if there's no one else in the shop.

*

I have dealt with today's post, today (yay!): a supermarket-chain promotion (green bin); an optician-chain promotion (dithered, but green bin); yet another tax-credits notification (corrected details and posted back – I have at least learned not to attempt to phone); and Trevor's leaflet (guess). Quick and easy. Day four is never a high-energy stage in any plan.

*

Jill and Trevor's place is abuzz with callers since he declared himself for election. I've never been inside their home, but I bet it's a pleasure to walk into. Not like ours. If you can force open our front door against the slag-heap of coats and carrier bags behind it, you will find little cheer and a general air of neglect. Plus there's always a bit of a smell (from what, I do not know). I wouldn't mind if I were a busy human-rights lawyer or a creative genius and therefore didn't make tidying up a priority, but it's quite humiliating when this is the state of our home and I am supposedly a full-time housewife. It's not even as if I sit about watching *Cash in the Attic*, drinking vodka out of a coffee mug – I'm battering about here all the time! I never sit down! How come it isn't all lovely?

I was so happy when we moved here. I sat on the old

paving slabs at the foot of the long garden, with my big, straight line of washing billowing in the sunny September breeze, looked up at this tall, grey house and believed this was the new start: I would always feel as carefree. But I have been ambushed over the hedge too many times by the good child next door, wanting to come and play with our unreliable rabble, whose bad noise announces our every homecoming to this quiet street. I have been ambushed too many times, too, by my face and hair and body reflected in the oven door, or the window, not looking at all strong and young and fresh as I had imagined when I stood by my laundry sails that bright day, future ahoy, hands on my self-satisfied hips, ignorantly flaunting my ugliness. So the garden turned out not to be the sanctuary it first had seemed, and we (I) have transformed this clean, bright-if-outdated house into a chipped, dark, jarring shell, full of awkward angles and unpleasantness.

*

The older children have retrieved Trevor's leaflet from the green bin, cut out his photo and stuck it to the lamp-post on their little brother's Happy Street, and now they can't stop laughing at themselves. Their sense of humour, when I have none and their father reserves his for adult people he cares to impress, is entirely their own triumph. It is also their gift to me. I love them.

*

(My lack of adult competence is also the reason I don't visit my elderly relatives and neighbours. You have to be the sort of bold, capable person who can barge in and start defrosting other people's freezers and know what to do about a commode, and that's not me. It must look like I can't be bothered, which isn't true. At heart, I'm very concerned about the vulnerability of the aged, but when it comes to making a practical job of it, I cannot see myself as . . . worthy. All I can feel is that I would be violating their privacy. Ditto wakes. I'm not shy of grief or washing-up, but I cannot go into the bereaved house because I never know whether to stand up and hand things round or take a seat and wait to be handed *to*. One option looks presumptuous of intimacy, the other presumptuous of status, and I don't want to be presumptuous at all, so I take the third option and send him over with a fruit loaf and a packet of teabags.

Except, of course, and this is 'Except' with a capital '*Ex*', I *can* visit the sick and attend the mourning on condition I do so as the guarded minion of Eleanor – goddess of tea, beneficence and organising people, and my supremely capable mother.)

*

Not only have I no colleagues to learn from, I also have no friends! Neat accomplishment! Abandoned *all* in exchange for him! No clue of the consequences. No clue at all.

*

I have been so lonely for so long that I regard it as normal now. And yet, and yet – I would like a friend. Could I be friends with the girl who looks like Joey Ramone? She's the first person I've seen round here who so obviously doesn't fit in (apart from Shouting Barbara and the guy who sits in the supermarket café wearing two hats – and, believe me, I've thought about taking my chances with them). I don't know where she lives, but it's probably quite near the roundabout, as she was walking there at eight thirty in the morning with her baby. She was walking on her own, so I'm hoping she's not already part of a mummy mafia, but anyway she didn't look the type.

* * *

Even Woods says he should never have married. Not just not married Wendy: Woods should never have married anyone. He is addicted to new love, I think. Which isn't really love at all, of course. What is the accurate term? (Not 'infatuation'. People only ever use 'infatuation' to describe someone else's feelings, never their own, so it's not a term to be trusted.) Woods enjoys the feeling of being with someone new to such an extent that he isn't willing to live without it. This is fair enough, I suppose. I really don't think he makes any promises to the women he meets these days, and they don't *have* to sleep with him (although, oddly, I can imagine that perhaps they feel they can't help it). The only real difficulty is that Woods had married Wendy before he had figured out these needs, and the two of them had already had a child together. I know it's too much to ask someone to live unhappily for the rest of his life because of a decision he made in his twenties, yet once you have a child it must become your overwhelming consideration, mustn't it? What makes it especially difficult to get comfortable with Woods's choice is that the particular thing he needs to be happy, and for which he has left his family, is *so* secular, so bodily, so self-indulgent. So sins of the flesh.

All this comes up now because I had to drive twenty-five miles on the motorway today (not my favourite thing) to collect a birthday present for Woods and Wendy's daughter. They both work during office hours, and I had gathered that the errand was creating difficulty, so I offered to fetch it for them, thinking it was just a local pick-up. But no. A big scary drive, then the whole six-lane ring-road thing and then another big, scary drive home. So Woods and Wendy have been on my mind.

I would love, love, love to fit our car with a super-powerful magnet for a rear bumper. How joyful I would be when the wankers who insist on driving an inch from my tail at sixty-five m.p.h. in the inside lane suddenly found themselves sucked right on to the back-end of our big, uncool estate car and unable to detach themselves.

The present for Woods and Wendy's daughter is an utterly beautiful rocking horse of a kind I have long wanted for our children. It stands as tall as me (I? Me? 'I', surely, for correct usage, but it still sounds a bit Noël

Coward. Who in this place would dare say, 'It stands as tall as I and can support a maximum weight of fourteen stones?' Not I. (Me.)). I couldn't possibly have lifted it into the car and felt choked with gratitude when the workshop assistant gently took the keys from my hand, flattened the back seats in a blink and heaved the horse into the space as lovingly as if it had been a living thing.

What a pity I made my bed before learning that a man with rough, blackened, sawdust-smelling hands can be angelically kind, while a man with soft, clean hands that smell of soap and ink can be harsh (and mean).

*

Thinking about it now, neither Woods nor Wendy could possibly have collected the horse in their cars. Woods drives a BMW saloon and Wendy a Toyota hatchback.

* * *

It pains me somewhat that the rocking horse we are now hiding for Woods and Wendy is something I have dreamed of for our family and, indeed, whose arrival has been stage-managed in my head for some time. I have it all worked out. Once the horse is prepared, the workshop (or a sympathetic neighbour) would hold it until the first night-time snowfall, at which time they would deliver it to our front doorstep, ring the bell and disappear. We adults would fake being otherwise engaged and ask the children to answer the door, where they would find the horse standing outside with an old-fashioned blanket over him and snow falling out of the dark sky on to the blanket and on to his mane and eyelashes. A note would be attached to the blanket, and they would open it, and it would say:

To whom it may certainly concern:

My previous owners have fallen into great danger.

They must flee and never return.

It is said there are noble children living within
these walls

and I am left here, therefore, to be entrusted to
their care.

I am a magical creature and thrive on love and warmth.

My name is Sebastian.

I have it all worked out, except how to pay for it. And any day now they are going to be too old.

It is my belief that every house in which children are to thrive should have three things: a rocking horse, a cuckoo clock and a piano. Needless to say, ours has none of the above.

*

I lost my morning queuing for holiday workshops for the children, so no post done today. Probably the beginning of the end of that particular plan, based on experience.

*

Where has all the old boldness gone? Is there a set amount dished out at birth and I used mine up too early? I hoard my remaining frugal ration like the last spoonful of rice, allowing myself just a grain a day to sustain me through the necessities. So tame, now. So careful. So beaten.

Would a piercing help? Would that constitute a small act of rebellion against the onslaught of blandness? Doubtful. Even at fifteen, I grasped the unfortunate irony of acts of copycat 'individualism'. Small, bejewelled mutilations are not the answer.

But what *is* the answer? There are plenty of books about *The Secret of My Success*, but none revealing *The Secret of My Failure*, which is the one I really need to get my hands on. Seemingly, the successful people have their winning ways all figured out, indexed and on sale for £8.99, while the failures just keep on bumping into the furniture.

Neither did I envisage a life of such social and sartorial timidity for my offspring. Thrilled when BBC2 'proved' that children are actually made of stardust, I nevertheless have to ask myself if stardust couldn't look better in something other than those awful ankle-gathered tracksuit bottoms and the crappy nylon T-shirt *tunics* they give away at sports camp.

Which is how, driving home from the supermarket, I was inspired with the idea that we could all register to take Native American middle names! (Perhaps Jeffrey Devine was playing Buffy St Marie.) We could do it at the start of the school holidays! It could be a thrilling new development in our sense of our identity! Which names would we choose? What would Jill and Trevor make of it?

(They would probably exchange a 'look', being too nice to snigger. But, hey, Jill and Trevor aren't the ultimate measure of lifestyle adventure. They might take their tall, handsome, confident selves and family on an overseas holiday every year, but it's always two weeks in *Spain* (the 'with chips' *Spain*, not the Hidden Planet), so they aren't quite up there with the Cousteaus/David Attenborough.)

Even the ankle-gathered tracksuits would look better on a kid called Running Bear.

I know all the words of 'Running Bear', as I know the words to all the songs on the *Fifties Favourites* album I owned as a child. We blame this for my annoying habit of shrieking, 'Name that band' every time a 1950s classic is used as a TV jingle. (You could go a 100 years without hearing The Platters and still pick them out from just three notes.) Another, similar, annoying habit is my interrupting of television programmes to point out which of the actors we have seen in which *other* programmes. At my worst, I compulsively point out minor screen moments of cast members of *The Archers*.)

So, of course, I started to sing 'Running Bear' in the car (Jeffrey Devine must have moved on to a talk strand), which also, of course, meant I quavered when I reached 'But the Water / [Tat-tat-tat]/ Was too wide / [Tat-tat . . . (tears)]'. It didn't *matter*. It's happened before ('Puff the Magic Dragon' while I was making the children's empty beds). Once you understand that life is, by nature, bitter-sweet, there's no going back.

A little weep on your own is one thing, though, but I'd

rather be one of those people fondly known to be easily moved to tears ('There she goes again . . . ') instead of being pettily embarrassed by individual witnessed episodes.

It can feel a bit wrong to cry just as readily at the end of *Toy Story* as when watching an African child nurse an AIDS-wasted parent. But I know, when I have my extra-wise head upon me, that the tears are all one, really.

*

A letter has come offering him his vasectomy on the NHS but at a private hospital, as a means to tackle the waiting list. I am unsure how to unravel this ethically. On the one hand, it engages with the depravity of private health care. On the other, it's the NHS that's inviting him to do it. Which wins?

*

Miss Morning, the School Principal, is taking early retirement. This is a loss to every child she will never teach. Ours were the lucky ones.

I know about Miss Morning's retirement because a note came home from school, but lots of the parents seem to be aware of all sorts of things that go on or supposedly go on in school, and I have no idea what they're talking about. I don't know where they get their information. Not from notes home, anyway.

*

Once again, I have spent the entire morning busy, yet our

domestic situation appears precisely as neglected and out of control as when I started. How, how, how can this be? What did I actually do?

*

I think it's because a lot of my work is invisible. For example, if I race round lifting the clothes off everybody's floors, but by the evening everyone has littered their patch afresh, my work there is invisible. If I grab all the dry laundry off the racks and radiators and fold it up and put it in the hot press (as with *'lavatory'*, I'd have preferred *'airing cupboard'*) but then immediately drape out today's almost identical wet washing, then both of these endeavours become invisible, too. If I tediously rehome each item in yesterday's Tidy Basket but then swiftly refill it with another day's detritus, who's going to know I did anything at all? And although I speed-sorted the truly frightening bits of post and dealt with them and updated the household accounts, you can't *see* that when you come in the front door, just as you can't see the energy that went into dashing off a shopping list, hurtling to the supermarket, flying up and down the aisles (in what I have worked out is the most time-efficient sequence), firing the shopping on to the conveyor belt and racing to beat the check-out assistant who wants to put potatoes and biscuits and jam jars all in one bag when I have a *system* (fridge bag, freezer bag, high cupboard, low cupboard, cupboard under the oven, etc.), which saves considerable time when it comes to putting away. What you *can* see, upon opening the front door, is all the things I *didn't* do – like Hoover (I'd have preferred 'vacuum', obviously), or dispose of any of those slag-heap carrier bags or clean the thickening cobwebs from around the top of the door curtain or the fingerprints off the light-switch fittings, or get a new bulb for the fish tank. Or make any tea.

But at least it's Friday. On Fridays I enjoy the illusion that, what with the weekend, there will somehow be more time, and I'll start catching up. (On Sundays, I harbour a similar illusion about there being more time, once everyone's back at school.)

*

My excitement about the exotic naming revived when I shared the idea with the children, although after I had suggested Running Bear and Little White Dove I was stuck for further examples. The eldest had heard Soaring Eagle, which sounds magnificent, and everyone wanted to name their little brother Little Bear, but then they started on Stinging Bee and Big Creepy Spider and thought they were very funny, and the whole thing got stupid. My Little Pony.

*

Dances with Wolves, that's another one, although in my case it's *Dances with Radio 2* now, and mostly I don't even dance.

*

33

The idea came back to me in bed, and I made the mistake of telling him. Ridicule, ridicule. Derision, derision. Definitely laughing *at*, not *with*, which at least prompted me with the perfect Native American name for him. Shite Hawk.

* * *

Rachel got in our car today! Normally I hate people unexpectedly getting in our car, or even opening the door and sticking their heads in, because the interior is so dirty. When it comes to cars, this bothers people much more than dirt on the outside. They pretend not to notice, which I now know is actually the most mortifying part, because it denies me the opportunity to say what I desperately need to say, which is that *I know. I know* other people clean the muddy shoe-prints off the carpet and the seat-backs from week to week. *I know* they Hoover the upholstery and remove the empty juice boxes, and *I know* other people's dashboards don't have *fur. I know* it's not supposed to smell like this. I am failing, yes, but I do *know.* (He says he can't smell anything but that if it bothers me so much I should buy one of those dangly Christmas trees. The unpleasant smell is bad, but not as bad as one of those evil, toxic little things.)

I was parked at the back gate of the school, and it was pouring with rain, and Rachel was just suddenly there, putting her little boy in the back seat with mine and saying, 'What's the stink?' Hurrah! Thus, I discovered the relief of *expressing* my anguish and explained that I could not eliminate the smell because I had been unable to track down its source.

Rachel said when it stops raining I should park the car in the driveway and open all its doors and just allow the fresh air to circulate for as long as possible. (He will go bonkers if he comes home from work to find all the car doors hanging open.)

It turns out Rachel is a single parent. Her older children go to our children's school, and they have all moved into a house nearby, so she can walk them there, with the little boy in the buggy. Rachel isn't sure if people in this town are going to take to her. Because she was so forthright, I asked her why she had smiled at us that day when he failed to give her right of way crossing the road. She said, 'I looked at you sitting up there beside him, and I looked at me out there on my own, and I thought, At least I don't have to live with you, you shit. Plus, these teeth cost me a fortune and I want to get my money's worth.'

For the first time in a very long while, I have the excited, bubbly feeling that I am about to have a friend. Rachel is the girl who looks like Joey Ramone.

* * *

My whole world is clutter. It's not just the postal backlog, it's everything. I would really be a lot happier as a minimalist. I would love to open my wardrobe doors to reveal nothing but two black T-shirts, two white T-shirts and two pairs of jeans. But it takes so long to get rid of all the excess, especially as the children don't like parting with anything. I came up with the compromise of camcording each item before it goes – which seemed brilliant at the time, but is, in practice, tremendously slowing – so if there are any regrets about discarding anything, we can bring out the recording and feel that we still sort of have it.

Perhaps I should camcord him.

*

When I first came to this town, I forced myself to read its weekly newspaper in an effort to get to know my community. Now that I feel I simply cannot face yet another giant-cheque ensemble or another councillor pointing at 'no fence' or 'no double yellow lines' or 'no dog-turd bin', I just look at the job and property ads and fantasise about a different life.

Of course, I am much too old to believe that Life Will Be All Right If Only . . . about anything. Certainly not If Only I had no postal backlog, or If Only I had a complete new wardrobe, or the right hair cut or a cash windfall, or if I lived in the country, or in a cave. Life will be all right if only I learn how to live it, that's all.

I used to think if only I could get the whole house really tidy and sorted out, with a place for everything and everything in its place, all would be well. But then I thought, The day that happens will be the day I find a lump.

*

As there is no point fretting over things I cannot change, I shall concentrate on those things I can. My new tool is going to be *Creative Visualisation*. I am *Creatively Visualising* my home, exactly as it is but with the postal backlog completely gone. Do I feel significantly different? Yes, I do. My home would feel like Disneyland if all my post were up to date. So that is what I am going to do. It's worth another try. Ten items a day. I can do it.

(And then I could *Creatively Visualise* other previously impossible tasks being successfully completed. I could visualise an empty ironing basket. Gleaming paintwork. The oven!)

*

Rachel didn't get in the car today. It wasn't raining.

* * *

I was unexpectedly summoned from my car into school at pick-up time today. Having hurried out from kitchen-cleaning operations, to which I would return, I had added only the speediest necessities for the drive and was thus obliged to traipse across the playground and through the building in stained purple tracksuit bottoms and zip-up winter ankle boots. Excruciating though this was, it could have been even worse – I was also sporting a vest top that exposed my unshaven armpits (worn without a bra, and, indeed, without a chest), and I offered up a godless prayer of thanks that I had hastily grabbed an old gardening shirt and stuck it on on my way out. I will never, ever do the school pick-up again wearing clothes in which even I am actually frightened to leave the car.

*

Eccentricity, so often beloved in a man, is invariably reviled in a woman. The later you figure this out, the more devastating the discovery. At least it is if you happen to be a woman. And eccentric. How did it take me so long to work out that there is no female equivalent to Columbo? He may be dismissed initially by the glamorous criminals he pursues, but they all come to respect him in the end, and the audience adores him. Columbo is definitely attractive. But put a *woman* out there slouching about, lighting cigar butts in a grubby, crumpled coat, and it won't matter how brilliant her mind, she will be a figure of disgust. Even Shouting Barbara is quite presentably turned out.

Miss Marple is asexual.

*

Would my life work better if I lowered my standards? Take my approach to cleaning the toilet – I cannot merely wipe the splashed rim, ever. I must approach, gloved up and in my pinny, toting a whole bucketful of cleaning paraphernalia. I start at the window sill and I work down, bagging up paper towels and disposable sponges as I go: over the cistern, the handle, the piping, the lid, the seat, the bowl, the base, more piping, the skirting board and the floor. I might not do the entire door, but I will do the door handle. I *would* do the door handle, but it fell off about two years ago so I do the bit where the door handle was. All this takes quite a while, so instead of doing it, I don't do it.

I cannot reaffix the toilet door handle because it is broken. I cannot replace the toilet door handle because it matches all the other upstairs door handles, and I can't find one the same anywhere, and we can't afford to replace all six. So the two pieces of broken handle sit on the third shelf of the book case on the landing, not high enough to fall on to anyone's head, and I dust round them.

(*Would* dust round them, if . . .)

It's no wonder I blink.

*

He is trying to have that night out with Woods again. I am a little concerned – with the house quiet, will I find myself listening for Pete and Stephanie's vibrator?

If I tell the boys to keep a look out for Woods, then go and find myself some busy job to do upstairs standing on a stool, I could avoid having to answer the door. Deciding on this plan now would save a lot of time and anxiety. (Although I will still waste *some* time running upstairs and climbing on to the stool every time I hear a car in the avenue.)

The early night will do me good. I think a good long rest away from the world will give my eyes time to settle.

*

Today I was in Rachel's house! She stuck her head through the car door when I was doing the first school pick-up, took a good sniff and said, 'That's definitely not as bad.' She invited me to drive her to her house and come in for a cup of tea. I have promised myself that I am going to try to stop saying, 'No', to things out of fear, so I said, 'OK'.

Rachel's house is, as I suspected, immaculate. When you stand at the front door you can see right to the back of the kitchen, and it's like something out of an advert. The window over the sink actually sparkles. There are bright, clean curtains. There is nothing on the draining board. A very clean dishcloth, folded in two, hangs over the gleaming mixer tap. There is nothing on the work surfaces, except what you want to be there – a fat kitchen roll on a shiny spindle, a matching mug tree with six identical mugs, a very clean-looking toaster and kettle set. There is a round table covered with a bright PVC cloth that matches the curtains, and there's nothing on that, either. Not even crumbs or sticky patches. The whole place smells of clean.

I would like to be one of those comfortable, self-assured people who saunter into someone's house and immediately put on the kettle and look round for the fridge, but I am not. I am the sort of person who, in Rachel's house today for the first time, admired everything just a bit *too* much, smiled a bit *too* hard with delight and for too long. I loved *everything*. Everything was *gorgeous*. I also did all this upright and awkward, with my coat still on, and as if my mother had told me not under any circumstances to touch anything in case I broke it.

Rachel told me to sit down and showed me a snapshot of her kitchen taken just before she moved in, three months ago. We have been in our house for three years, and any current picture of our kitchen would need a lot of airbrushing to look as good as her 'Before' shot.

Rachel gave each of our two boys a beaker of Ribena with a lid, opened the back door and steered them out. 'Fully enclosed, no dogs, no cats, no poisonous plants, shed locked,' she said to me, giving me the slightly creepy feeling that my mind had just been read, but she explained, 'I do child minding. I know all the worries.'

Rachel's daddy tiled her kitchen and fitted her new cupboard doors and worktops. I tried to imagine my father fitting cupboard doors, and failed. Rachel painted the walls herself and put down the floor tiles, and she got a man in to wire the new lighting. She made it sound easy, but I know it isn't. But she really did make it *sound* easy.

Rachel doesn't have any children to mind here, yet, because she arrived in the middle of the school year. But now that she's fixed up the kitchen and the bathroom and the garden, she's going to put an ad in the classifieds.

Rachel is prettier close up than from a distance. Her skin is sort of translucent, and her hair is sleek and shiny, not frizzy like Joey Ramone's. In fact, I don't think she is aware of any passing resemblance to a New York godfather of punk: she just doesn't like having to wear glasses and is trying to make a feature of them.

When it was time to go, Rachel said she'd take a lift as far as the post office, and we put her boy's buggy in the boot. Seeing the space in the back of our estate car, Rachel said: 'That's good to know . . . '

* * *

In the post office this morning, which was partly to do with my ten-items-a-day policy and partly to do with hoping to bump into Rachel, I bumped into my own stupidity instead. And I really didn't see it coming. I had (kindly, I thought) picked up a Good Luck In Your New Life greetings card for a friend of our children who has emigrated to Dubai. I had also (cleverly, I thought) taken it to the counter for weighing so that I could purchase appropriate stamps, attach these and pass on the card for posting by the uncle still living here who would know the interim Dubai arrangements and where best to send it. Everything was fine until the counter assistant asked me: 'Where is Dubai?'

Everyone assumes everybody else knows what we're all talking about, but neither I nor the Royal Mail employee nor the poor gormless (and now alarmed) boy using the next window could answer the question. I had thought I knew, until actually confronted, at which point the phrase 'United Arab Emirates' popped into my head – but was that a country or countries? Or a state or states within a country? Was *Dubai* a city in a state or in a country? Or was it, in fact, itself a state or even a nation? I've been using the word 'Dubai' on and off for years, without actually knowing what I'm talking about.

And when did people you turn to for help start being younger than yourself? That poor gormless boy. When, in desperation, I looked to the next customer for salvation, I believe I really expected to find a barrel-chested, hairy-armed man standing there with the answer. Why?

*

The Creative Visualisation is going well, in terms of the post tray. Unfortunately, to prioritise this, everything else has had to slide. That's the problem with prioritising – it assumes that some of the stuff you were previously doing didn't really matter. But what if it *all does*? I need to prioritise the post, because it hangs like gloom and, if not challenged, rages out of control. However, I also need to prioritise laundry, because we all need a supply of clean clothes, and someone must maintain this. It is also important to eat properly, so shopping and cooking must be done and packed lunches put together. And, of course, it is perilous to store, prepare or eat food in unsanitary conditions, so kitchen-cleaning is vital, as is cleaning of the bathroom and WC. Keeping the place at an acceptable level of cleanliness and tidiness generally is important, too, of course, if a house is to feel like a home and a comfortable place into which to welcome visitors, but equally important is keeping on top of your finances – exceeding your overdraft limit is a costly business and a worrying one, and insurances must be kept current. And then there's personal hygiene – yours and your children's – and giving support with homework and hobbies. There's dejunking, so your life doesn't get jammed with clutter, and taking all the recyclables to the dump. So far, so important. But that's just the practicalities (and not even all of them). Then there are the relationships – we're supposed to prioritise those as well. Quality time with the children every day. Quality time with our partners. *When? When?* Popping in on elderly relatives, staying in touch with our friends. (. . . ?) And what about the exercise we're meant to be taking for our health and longevity and for the Prozac-like endorphins? What about the attention we must pay, if we are to thrive as properly engaged, thinking people, to developments in politics, the environment and the arts? Aren't we supposed to read a few of the new books? The occasional newspaper? This doesn't even include the indisputably important activities of attending your GP, your hospital clinics, your dentist – who tells you to make *flossing* a priority! And, according to *Good Housekeeping*, it's an *absolute must* to prioritise '*Me Time*'. *Who* Time?

*

I decided to prioritise the hall, because the feelings of shame every time I have to open the front door are exhausting. Success! I might only have moved my clutter problem sideways into another room, but perhaps this is the right approach sometimes, if it buys you a little space.

Perhaps this is what other people do all the time. Perhaps everyone else has a secret Dorian Gray room where all the evil festers so that the public rooms can be kept beautiful.

*

Trevor's election campaign is gathering momentum. He has mobilised a squad of his Youth Soccer colleagues to knock on doors. This could be rather shrewd, as his big election issue is getting the youth off the streets and into organised activities. However, there is absolutely no evidence whatsoever of any youth *on* the streets in this town. As far as I can see, they're all at home in their centrally heated bedrooms playing PlayStation and revising for their ASs. Trevor is exploiting inappropriate tabloid-generated anxieties for votes.

I opened the door and practically dragged the Youth Soccer person inside to witness the clean and tidy hall. In exchange, I felt I had to accept the leaflets he gave me from his clipboard, although I would never, could never, vote for Trevor's party. The rosette-wearer will have left our house supposing that the 90 per cent of it he didn't see was as immaculate as the small bit he did. Is successful housekeeping actually mainly trickery?

I was also *not* thrown into a complete panic when Woods called unexpectedly (that is to say, *I* wasn't expecting him) – he never comes in any further than the hall.

Not only does Woods not vote, but he manages to make me feel small-minded for doing so. And the more passionately I want to remind him about the privilege of universal suffrage and the comparisons with other, less democratic times and places, the more petty and tight-arsed my inner voice sounds to me, so I say nothing. Woods can take the greatest achievements of mankind and make you feel they are the pedantic concerns of a few self-righteous agitators, meanwhile somehow giving his own sensual self-indulgent way of life an air of greatness. He does all this without saying a word.

*   *   *

Someone has vandalised Trevor's election poster. The one on the roundabout. They have added a moustache and written 'Gay' in black marker. Presumably this is the action of a disaffected young person for whom Trevor is determined to provide more Youth Soccer.

I need a new black marker.

(*Not* for vandalising purposes.)

*   *   *

While I was quietly lying on the bed doing a Creative Visualisation exercise, I heard next door's vibrator start to whir again. Pete works shifts, so sometimes he's at home in the day. Stephanie does *not* work shifts. There were no voices. I left the room. I am uncomfortable with my imaginings.

*

I have bought a new black marker, a fine liner and a page-a-day desk diary. Now I must remember that these are merely the means, not the end.

* * *

Round at Rachel's again today, between pick-ups. As we were driving down her cul-de-sac, we met Wendy. She stopped alongside us and put down her window, so I stopped and put down mine. Wendy said to me (although she was taking a good, appraising look at Rachel), 'Thanks for collecting Billie's horse. She loves it.' I said she was very welcome, but inwardly I was slightly disappointed that they had given it to her already, as it isn't her birthday until tomorrow. I asked Wendy about her new *ergonomic* kitchen. Rachel said, 'What's an ergonomic kitchen when it's at home?' But Wendy couldn't quite keep the condescension out of her tone when she answered, 'It means everything is where you want it, when you want it,' and Rachel dropped her chin and murmured into her cleavage, 'Might as well have it in the kitchen – you didn't get it in the husband.' So now it must seem I've been gossiping, which I have not. How does Rachel know Woods and Wendy?

*

It's not just *one* of Trevor's posters – it's all of them. I suppose if you pursue a life in public office, however parochial, you inevitably set yourself up as a target.

47

Trevor's not a new born baby – he will have been prepared for such things, I dare say. But I hate the thought of his little children being upset by seeing their daddy's image violated. Sadly for them all, I suspect theirs is a home in which, like the vandal's, 'Gay' is an accusation.

* * *

Rachel's children don't eat biscuits in her house, ever, because of the crumbs. She told them when they were very young that people only eat biscuits indoors when they are visiting at someone *else's* house, and they accepted this. I thought they were bound to work out that 'someone else's house' must constitute home for that someone, who was therefore eating biscuits in their own home and thus proving Rachel's assertion untrue. She said, 'Paul [their father] was as thick as shite. My kids'll *never* figure that out.'

I am going to invite Rachel round to our house, but I am not going to make a big special effort for her because (a) it would take me until July to get everything tidied up, and (b) I am so tired of pretending to everyone out there that everything inside is all right when it's not. The tension between the fixed smile and the hidden decay is exhausting. I want to be honest with Rachel, if with no one else, and I think perhaps I can risk it.

*

The leg has come off my glasses. I look like Jack Duckworth.

*

Jill and Trevor appear in eight photographs in today's local paper. There is a big colour portrait of Jill, tanned and smiling in the Youth Soccer strip and Salt-of-the-Earth rosette (she is very photogenic).There is also: Jill and Trevor presenting the Table Tennis Cup at the Riverside Drop-In Youth Centre Trevor and Jill visiting inmates of the Sleepy Valley retirement home; Trevor shaking hands with the managing director of the uPVC window factory which is sponsoring the new under-13s league; Trevor pointing at 'no pedestrian crossing' between the elderly people's Fold accommodation and the post office; Jill awarding the prize for the most interesting teapot (I am not kidding) at a meeting of the Ladies' Circle; Trevor and Jill and the children among a large group shot of their annual sunday-school outing; and Trevor, Jill, *Pete and Stephanie* (!) and others, all wearing rosettes, and captioned, 'Trevor and his campaign team still smiling despite the blisters after burning shoe leather all this week.'

I didn't know Trevor and Jill and Pete and Stephanie were friends, who did things together. I thought they just shouted, 'Hi!' and 'All right?' to each other if they happened to be outside their houses at the same time, getting into or out of their cars. Like they do with us.

*

Marilyn Softly has left him a message on our call minder, which, of course, he returned immediately. (Some of his saved messages are weeks old and will never be returned,

49

but they aren't from people who Matter.) Marilyn is having a farewell party for Miss Morning, the school principal, and wants him to make a speech. He will make a good speech. It will be funny and mischievous, and anyone who hasn't heard him speak before, or who hasn't Mattered enough to see more than the surly side of him, will remark on what a talent he has. (Marilyn Softly is the special needs co-ordinator at school. She is tall, blonde and gorgeous. It is clear that quite a few of the daddies wouldn't mind her helping them with a few special needs of their own.) I think he could probably have had a career in public speaking, if he'd known the right turns to take. I think he sometimes wonders how he didn't end up as a full-time entertainer instead of deputy editor of *Go for It* magazine, the monthly trade journal for small-business proprietors.

* * *

I brought Rachel into our house. Having spent the weekend blinking increasingly wildly at the thought of it, I couldn't bear to have put my poor eyes through all that trauma for nothing. If I hadn't done it this time, I'd have had to go through the whole crippling apprehension process again. So I asked her, and she came.

I did warn her, but in the knowledge that *everyone* apologises in advance for 'the state of the place', even though the greatest sin evidenced in most of their very nice homes is a basket of unironed laundry in the corner, or the sofa cushions having missed their daily plump.

By the time I put the key in the front door, my heart was thudding and my armpits exuding so much fear it was surprising several rats didn't break from their sewer pipes and leap at my throat.

Once inside, Rachel could not quite disguise her discomfort with the general gloomy grottiness of the place. I could feel her thinking, Why don't you just tidy up? The very fact that Rachel, *Rachel*, was maintaining a discreet silence, said more than words. But she gamely ploughed through the kitchen, past the breakfast things still on the sticky table, past the murky, unlit fish tank, the spilling piles of post and the sprawl of dirty washing gathered on the floor and began to make a cup of tea. Rachel, who doesn't have a filter jug, filled the kettle from the tap, and then opened the wall-cupboard above, looking for biscuits (she was, after all, visiting in someone else's house). 'Christ!' Rachel said.

Inside the cupboard, all the biscuit tins are lined up facing the front, with big white stickers saying in clear black letters:

Lunchbox Treats	**Shortbread**
Ice Cream Accessories	**Chocolate Biscuits**
Biscuits	**Crackers (open)**
Cake	**Crackers (sealed)**

There is also a large round Roses chocolates tin, labelled '*Christmas Cake*', and a square, purple Cadbury's Biscuit

Selection one, with a winter village scene, labelled '*Mince Pies*'. (Of course, these are empty in May.) Plus, there is a large cafetière; a small cafetière; three bags of ground, decaffeinated, organic, Fair Trade coffee; three jars of instant, decaffeinated, organic, Fair Trade coffee; three boxes of decaffeinated, organic Fair Trade teabags; two packets of loose, organic, Fair Trade Earl Grey tea and a battery-operated milk-frother. There are also two little muslin pouches swinging on the inside of the door, containing a tablespoon of fresh, dry, ground coffee and a tablespoon of Earl Grey tea, making the cupboard smell permanently gorgeous. All these items fill the space perfectly, so it is easy to maintain.

Rachel swung round to look at me, as if she was going to speak, but she didn't. She shut the cupboard doors and opened the next nearest one, under the worktop. Lined up there, in tightly lidded boxes of varying sizes are, '*Dry Goods, Savoury*', '*Dry Goods, Sweet*' and '*Stock Cubes, Sauce Mixes and Seasonings*', plus one of those cardboard wine-carriers you can get from the supermarket, containing olive oil, extra-virgin olive oil, white-wine vinegar, soy sauce, an open bottle of red wine with a wine-saver top on it and a screw-top bottle of cooking sherry.

Rachel opened the larder. From front to back, the larder is the depth of four tins, with two tins' height per shelf. From left to right stand: eight tins of baked beans, eight tins of soup arranged in four matching pairs, eight tins of coconut milk, four jars of green pesto on top of four jars of red, five packets of tomato passata (fits the same space), eight tins of tuna *stacked behind* six tins of sardines. Next shelf: eight tins of creamed rice, eight tins of creamed semolina, eight tins of custard, four tins of pineapple (odd size), four tins of raspberries on top of four tins of fruit cocktail, four packets of meringues (lying down, fill the same space), two packets of trifle sponges. There is a little gap at the end where I used to keep packets of jelly, but getting jelly without the bad E numbers has proved impossible and that is why there is a gap.

'*Jesus,*' Rachel said. She closed the doors and looked at the floor, then at me. 'You're meant to hide all the crap in the cupboards, not . . . !' She looked around at my domestic disorder with something like despair. Then she said, 'Your life is fucking inside out.'

* * *

Rachel and her children are going on holiday to Spain. The day after tomorrow! Rachel found it on Teletext. It takes me most of a year to prepare to go on holiday and is one of my topmost stressful events per annum. (The others are Christmas and each of the children's birthday parties.) Rachel has the same number of children as me. How does she do it?

*

I am going to try to be a good friend, and a giver, not a taker. I am going to put together three little travel packs for

Rachel's children, for the journey, to help keep them occupied. They are flying, so everything must be compact. I could buy mini-markers and little scribble pads, and those tiny packs of modelling clay, and the little red fortune-teller fish that curl up in your hand, and a Freddo Frog and a Milky Bar each, and a few euro. I could pack them into three travel belts, and that would keep their hands free for getting on and off the plane.

*

The first time I was in Spain it was in San Sebastian, and my cigarette packet blew off the seafront-café table and sailed down on to the rocks and water far below. Because I had disastrously been doubling up my fag packet as my wallet for all my paper pesetas, I experienced that specific desolation felt only when you have irretrievably lost something like money that, while not human or even a pet, brings its own peculiar and terrible sense of grief. Then I realised that all those pesetas were equivalent to about £1.65, and it was such a relief.

Every afternoon in San Sebastian, when the tide started coming in, the sunbathers edged their towels and deck-chairs back and back towards the sea wall. And every day the tide just kept coming, so their towels and chairs and legs and footwear were soaked and they had to run for the steps. How could this happen day after day? Were they the same people, thinking, 'Maybe this time . . . '? Or was it a fresh batch every afternoon, who couldn't learn from the mistakes of others or believed it would simply be different for them?

I had another but quite different lucky escape travelling in Denmark (aeons later), where we presumptuously took the children on holiday without knowing a single word of the language. We were even pronouncing the name of the airline incorrectly (although Dan-air does look as though it would be pronounced 'Dan-air' and not, as it is in fact, correctly, 'Den-air')! I cannot stop being grateful that, in a fit of 'abroad' confidence, I enquired on our first day the Danish expression for 'thank you' and learned that it is 'tak'. *Because*: on our last night, in a McDonald's 'restaurant' in Copenhagen, I saw 'tak' on all the self-service bins. Given my self-esteem issues, had these first and last experiences happened the other way round (as they so easily could), I would have spent my entire Denmark experience believing that everyone we met was smirking 'Rubbish' at me and my family.

*

My kids taught Rachel's kids the Things-That-Should-Be-Available-On-Prescription-But-Aren't game, which was a big hit! Between them they came up this time with: Wagon Wheels, Alton Towers, *Father Ted*, fudge, McFlurries, being pushed on a swing, hot-water bottles, motor homes and bungee bouncing.

*

55

Rachel is right. My life *is* fucking inside out. How has this happened? And what can I do?

* * *

I went round to Rachel's house uninvited for the first time because, for once, I felt I might actually be able to help. *With what?* The dishcloth was still neatly folded on the mixer tap, the window still sparkled. Rachel, looking fresh as a daisy, has the cases packed and ready to lift. The only thing she still has to sort out before she leaves is a new pair of sunglasses. How does she do it? Does she stay up all night? The day before I go on holiday I am grey with anxiety. I am surrounded by lists and bags of clothing, medication, back-up medication, towels, washing stuff, coats of various properties, spare shoes, woolly hats, sunblock, maps, directions, telephone numbers, documentation. I cannot rest for fear of Leaving Something Behind. I am screaming at the children, who are starting to wear the clothes that I am trying to pack. I am screaming for some back-up or we won't be ready at all. Every year I swear that this time, this time I will make a master list so that preparations for every future expedition will run like clockwork, but, at crisis point, there isn't time, and when we get back I'm too exhausted and just want to put it behind me. Our dishcloth will *never* hang neatly on the tap. Our house will be abandoned in all its usual filth and squalor, just festering until our return. I gave Rachel the three little travel packs. She seemed . . . 'bemused', I think (although I sometimes wonder if Rachel's emotions are as subtle as my vocabulary for them). I am giving them a lift to the airport. It will be at four thirty tomorrow morning, so my own children will still be safely asleep in bed, and even *I* cannot foresee the emergency they might create in their sleep that even *he* couldn't deal with for *one and a half hours*. There will be virtually no traffic, so I'm not even worried about the motorway.

* * *

Rachel says when she gets back from her holiday she will give me a hand to get my house straightened up. On reassessing the housekeeping situation, now revealed as completely wrongly prioritised (i.e., 'inside out'), it seems to me that I need to think in terms of certain Core Tasks which will (a) keep all the basics ticking over, and (b) avoid embarrassment if unexpected callers arrive. These Core Tasks are: Evening Meal, School Uniforms, Packed Lunches, Basic Kitchen Hygiene, Basic Bathroom Hygiene, Basic WC Hygiene, Basic Downstairs WC Hygiene, Essential Laundry, Essential Shopping. If these are not in place, however well labelled the biscuit tins, life breaks down quite quickly.

*

What will I wear to Miss Morning's leaving do?

*

How have I ended up with absolutely no going-out clothes? I have tracksuit bottoms and cardigans for housework and jeans with the same cardigans for school-runs and shopping. I have zip-up boots for when it's wet, *faux*-suede trainers for when it's not and slippers for indoors. I do have one blue dress which, until recently, I still thought of as my 'new' dress, although it is now fifteen years old and has served for every wedding and christening in its lifetime. But it wouldn't go round my fat tummy these days, and the matching shoes wouldn't go round my fat feet.

*

How miserable all that sounds, and I'm not miserable at all. Not about a few bloody clothes, anyway!

*

Actually, I may be jumping the gun a bit. No one has actually said I am invited to Miss Morning's leaving do. And there hasn't been a note home from school.

* * *

It said on *All in the Mind* today that when questioned about the probability of various bad things happening to them, depressed people assessed the likelihood with greater accuracy than did 'normal' people. The 'normal' people were mistakenly optimistic, compared to the hard statistics, about their chances of being afflicted in various ways. *Do you see what this means?* The so-called 'illness' of so-called 'depressed people' is, in fact, a sound grasp of reality, for which the 'cure' is to lure them away from this and into a deluded state. The so-called 'sane' people are living in a fantasy land. (No wonder suicide rates are so high among psychiatrists.)

I am not being funny, but I already knew this and could have told 'them' without the expense of some massive study. (Lots of people could – all so-called 'depressed' people, for a start.) How many times have I heard the results of another new 'study' and thought, I could have told them that! At such moments, I become a maniac disgruntled citizen and wonder exasperatedly why 'they' don't put the money into curing cancer, which I *don't* know how to do. I also think lots of ordinary people (especially the 'depressed' ones who, as it turns out, have the best grounding in reality) should be brought into the research loop where scientists just aren't cutting it. There is great merit in a 'fresh eye' and in the ideas that people can only bring to the table *because* they can't even start to think on the same tracks as the 'experts'. (I *know* about the mixed metaphor, but I haven't *time* to fix it.) For example, I know that human sperm, applied to warts, cures them. But who can I tell that to? What would that think tank be called? (I'm not sure the Department of Health plays Things That Should Be Available On Prescription But Aren't.)

*

There is going to be a massive anti-poverty rally. This is where my realism, even though it has now been validated by 'experts', melts. I still believe we can save all the starving babies if we try hard enough. I believe we can rise up and stand together and bond with our fellow humans and demand that we stop stop stop prevaricating, sinning by omission, looking the other way, buying more leather sofas and sleigh beds and decking, while walking cadavers haul themselves dusty miles for the possibility of a dish of gruel.

*

I have made out a rota of my Core Tasks so that everything gets the appropriate slice of time each day, thus ensuring all chores get completed. Today was cleaning the bathroom and upstairs WC, which I have done, but, of course, I must also shop for the evening meal and packed lunches and prepare these and keep pushing the laundry through.

*

I am getting sick of Sellotaping this leg back on to my glasses. Even if I do get something new to wear to the leaving do, I'm still going to be sporting these. Still no note home about it, and I haven't even overheard any school-gate whisperings.

*

Once upon a time, I imagined I would be the sort of woman who boldly took her children on rallies, probably involving baby slings and beads and dungarees and faces painted with rainbows and butterflies. If I *had* grown into that sort of mother, perhaps they would already have names like Clear Water and Deer Jumping Downhill (I've been looking them up). But why *don't* we go to the rally?

Although I strongly expect him to ridicule me for suggesting it, I might be wrong. There was a time . . .

*

No, there wasn't.

* * *

Oh. My. God. Trevor is all over the Sunday papers, and this time it has nothing to do with a giant cheque. Trevor has visited a masseur in a hotel, and the masseur has gone to the papers with photos and texts he saved on his mobile phone. Trevor has issued a statement to the effect that he was receiving treatment for a sports injury and this was a privately run clinic, but the general buzz seems to be that either his injury was in the region of his prostate or Trevor is being disingenuous.

Pete and Stephanie have taken Trevor's party rosette off their car. I wonder what went through Pete's mind, given his own daytime vibrating proclivities.

* * *

He needs glasses! He is horrified, because he thinks of it in terms of ageing. I am horrified because his firm is going to pay for his glasses because he works on a computer screen, so he will have his new glasses in his hand on Wednesday, while I, who have been wearing glasses since childhood, and *the same pair for eight years*, but am not employed by a *firm*, will have my new glasses when we win the lottery or the children's feet stop growing. He related this news actually *while* I was sticking the leg back on to *my* frames with Sellotape, *again*, as if the sight of it had just reminded him.

*

Trevorgate continues. He went on Zero FM today, after his party suspended him pending an inquiry. He said it's all a big misunderstanding, and I suppose it is: Trevor misunderstood what is likely to happen next when an aspiring elected representative espousing family values has gay sex with a stranger.

Although Trevor is behaving like a bit of an idiot, I feel sorry for him. I feel sorry for the teasing his kids will get at school.

Can Trevor still stand for election if he's suspended? Can he stand independently of the Salt-of-the-Earths if they don't want him? He's only got ten days until polling, and he's going to have to get together a new campaign. It's hard to see how he could continue on the youth-work ticket in a town where people don't register any difference between a homosexual and a sex offender.

I suppose the poster vandal is thinking, Told you so!

*

Did my Core Tasks. Hooray for me.

* * *

Life is full of irony. My head is so busy, it brought to mind 'Maybe I Think Too Much' by Paul Simon, which immediately made me think of the *Hearts and Bones* album generally, and the criticism of it, and how I really like it even though the smart money deemed it a failure, and I thought about René and Georgette Magritte giving their dog a surreal name (Après la Guerre) and how dogs react to the first syllable of their name anyway, so anything after that is unnecessary to the dog and therefore merely for the indulgence of the owner, and how naming dogs is really a kind of affectation, then, and naming a dog *surreally* certainly is, but how I really can quite like affectation in others; and it doesn't stop there, because then I thought of the people who bought me this album and wondered where they are now, and how we lost touch, and how I lose touch with everyone, and is this just normal or am I a bad friend, and was that only in the past or will I look back one day on how I lost touch with Rachel, or – *horror!* – how I lost touch with *my children?* (Could that happen?) 'Maybe I Think Too Much'. Look what that started. So *is* life full of irony, or is it just mine?

*

Nothing ages the female soul quite like the acquisition of a gynaecological case history. The Sleeping Beauty went to sleep for 100 years and was awoken by a prince's kiss. I went to sleep for twelve years and woke up as Les Dawson. I'll have to go back to the doctor.

*

Trevor's kids have vanished. Their bikes are gone from the driveway and I don't see any sign of them in the avenue after school. I'm guessing they have gone to stay with their other granny.

*

Did Core Tasks. Yippee.

* * *

Why do I blink like this? It's not as simple as a faulty reflex, because that would have no emotional pay-off, and this has. The little bit of over stretching to the tiny muscles when I suddenly clench my eyes is a compulsion, with the dark gratification that entails. It lies half way between the voluntary and involuntary, between the conscious and unconscious, like swallowing. Very like swallowing, in fact, and sometimes it moves to my swallow, to flexing that other muscle at the front of my throat. Why all the vulnerable places? If I'm going to do this, why couldn't it be somewhere strong? (Then, instead of being a compulsion, I could call it 'toning'.) But, instead, I flex and flex some little place until it hurts, and then I have to try to ration myself in case I do physical damage: just one more hard blink . . . just one more . . . just one more. Something tells me I know what it really is, even though I'm still kidding myself I can fix it with cold teabags and an aromatherapy candle.

*

Trevor has said he will stand for election somehow. One of his staunchest supporters went on the Zero FM phone-in today and said that the whole masseur scandal was actually a scam stage-managed by Trevor's enemies. He says all the local election candidates received phone texts from this so-called masseur, and it was just unlucky that Trevor, a keen footballer, was the one who happened to have a legitimate sports injury so thought it worthwhile to avail himself of the proffered service. He said Trevor is going to sue the Sunday papers.

*

Where on earth does *he* get his ideas from these days? According to him, the anti-poverty rally is basically going to be a riot organised by anarchists and quelled by mounted police and the riot squad, probably using water cannon. Jesus. One of the prime movers behind this event is *Christian Aid*! Is he going to start boycotting their subversive soup-and-cheese luncheons in the church hall next? He says 'anarchist' like it's something so sinister. What's an anarchist, anyway, but someone who has more faith in my inherent goodness than I have myself? Someone who believes that, even without the legal obligations and red tape, I would still choose to behave like a decent human being.

*

Did Core Tasks, except for bathroom and WC, as I ran out of time. Should be OK from yesterday, though.

*

His glasses are quite nice.

* * *

Rachel and family fly back today. They could be in the air right now. I don't know how they're getting home from the airport. I thought about phoning up for their arrival time and going to meet them, but there wouldn't be enough room in the car along with my own children. And, anyway, Rachel didn't say anything to me about getting home, and I don't want her to feel like I'm stalking her.

I have thought and thought about asking Rachel if we could go together to the anti-poverty rally and bring all our kids. I don't know. Could I live with myself if it really did turn ugly?

*

Cleaned kitchen thoroughly so I have somewhere to bring Rachel, should she call round, so no time left for Core Tasks, except for Evening Meal.

* * *

How does Rachel do it? The day after I arrive back from holiday, I stumble fuzzily about the house putting away the essentials, like medication, and undertaking only the absolute necessities, like providing meals. It could take me up to a week to do the holiday laundry and ages to unpack and put away everything 100 per cent. Rachel, however, was back at her spotless kitchen table today, with her cup of tea and her cut-price holiday cigarettes and new lighter, and everything is ship shape. She has already unpacked *everything*. She has washed and tumble-dried *everything*. She does not have a bundle of postcards she didn't get around to posting and will hang around the kitchen for weeks before disposal; nor does she have piles of sun-cream bottles and washbags and money-belts sitting on the bottom stair. Her post-holiday housekeeping is confirmation of all my suspicions that other people's homes do not look or function like mine. When I put this to Rachel, she cited the children's travel packs as the situation in microcosm. (She didn't use the word 'microcosm'.) According to Rachel, while my idea of a diverting package involves gathering lots of fiddly little components, hers is just a large bag of Haribos. I sort of understand the point she was making, about cutting corners and doing things the easy way, but I still don't know how to make that work for *me*. Cutting corners is OK, but what if the bits of life which you consider utterly essential are positioned right *on* the corners? I cannot start giving my children kilo bags of artificially coloured gummy sweets, even if it means I would get the washing and ironing done.

*

Rachel was delighted to learn that I live in the same avenue as Trevor Two-ways (as he is now widely known). Seemingly, news of his downfall was the talk of Alicante. I was unable to furnish Rachel with any details of his misdemeanour which she didn't already have, but she wanted to know all about Jill, for whom she feels sorry. Rachel does not seem to understand that the act of feeling *sorry* for Jill is a means of associating Jill with the 'offending' behaviour, in which she had no part. You cannot go around presuming to feel sorry for people on the basis of things their *spouses* have done. To do so is to insist that they become part of a transaction into which they did not enter. That is the beginning of the end. For the first time, I felt unnerved by Rachel because she doesn't seem to have any rigour of thought. Simultaneously, and arising from the same issue, I see that she considers *me* to be hopelessly unworldly (which all depends on how you measure worldliness: I was not the one who mistook a headline about the Israeli president Ariel *Sharon* for a story about Sharon out of *EastEnders*).

*

I mentioned to Rachel the possibility of going to the anti-poverty rally, but apparently that was the other talk of Alicante – how the rally is going to be an anarchist-led riot.

*

Rachel brought home a load of cheap Spanish cigarettes, which she doesn't even really like. I urged her to consider changing to lower tar when they're finished. She said, 'What, and I'll only get cancer lite?'

*

He says everyone will be assuming I am invited to Miss Morning's leaving do because he has been asked to speak at it, but he's wrong. He speaks at lots of things, and nobody expects to see me there. Occasionally I get invited, but I don't go. Partly because of lack of babysitters, but also because I went to one or two such functions in the early days and discovered my role was about as worthwhile as that of Cully Barnaby from *Midsomer Murders*, so now I don't bother.

*

Core Tasks nil, because I spent the morning at Rachel's. The upstairs WC now stinks of wee, again, instead of Ecover and tea-tree oil. We had an Indian takeaway for tea.

* * *

The one paper that didn't 'expose' Trevor last Sunday is giving his 'exclusive' account today. The headline is '"I'LL SUE" vows brave Trev', and it's all about how he's going to take the Sunday papers *and* the Salt-of-the-Earth Party to court and how the whole thing is a plot for which his party has inexplicably fallen, and how his family and close colleagues know the truth about what a wholesome, upright, youth-footballing kind of guy he is. He's going to stand on Thursday as an independent candidate. I'd vote for him if I didn't think he and the Salts would soon come running open-armed towards each other if he manages to get himself elected. Who else would you vote for round here? Local thinking on human rights, for example, extends to the right to a proper indoor shopping mall with late-night opening, instead of just a sort of canopied area between Benetton and the home bakery. We do not have environmental issues because we do not have an environment – that's something for people who went to university and watch Channel 4 – we just have 'outside'. I will vote, of course, because of the suffragettes and Nelson Mandela, etc., and because I never want to become complacent like Woods about the privilege of democracy, but the choices are: Trevor, a slightly lefter version of Trevor, a slightly righter version of Trevor and a female Trevor. Take your pick.

* * *

You can't turn on the telly or open a newspaper without being reminded of the mayhem when protesters rallied outside the World Trade Organisation conference in Seattle. They're all using that picture of a gas-masked 'anarchist' dressed in black with flames behind him, and everyone seems obliged to mention that the protest closed down all the Starbucks' coffee houses, which were apparently the ultimate symbol of 'Seattle life' (whatever that means). One of our children still occasionally needs his inhaler, plus I do not know whether studies have established any long-term damage done by one-off childhood exposure to CS gas. If the press are trying to manipulate me, they're doing a good job.

But I also remember when one of the children got a globe from the Early Learning Centre how shocked I was to discover that Seattle (*Frasier* – people like me, surely, only rich, attractive and witty) is actually further away from us than Rwanda (genocide, starvation, orphan epidemic, AIDS). Repeat: Rwanda is much closer to my house than *Frasier* in Seattle is; Rwandans are my nearer neighbours than the Cranes.

*

Tall, blonde Marilyn Softly came out of the back gate of school and got into our car today while I was waiting for the children. (I immediately started to sweat.) She said, in a conspiratorial tone, that she supposes she and my husband should be getting together to organise themselves for this do and asked if I knew whether it would be convenient to 'borrow' him on Thursday night. Marilyn's voice has a permanent laugh in it, like a ringing bell, as if everything she thinks and says is infused with mischief. I wonder how she will cope if ever asked to read a biblical text at a funeral. I agreed cooperatively to pass on the message, although I do find it strange that someone suggests making party plans on election night. Doesn't anybody think voting and the emergence of election results are special any more?

I was slightly stung when Rachel rolled up with her buggy and stood talking to Marilyn outside my car door instead of talking to me. It is so easy for Marilyn to strike

up a conversation with someone because she knows all of
our children.

*

I am spending too long on these Core Tasks, which is why
I keep running out of time. I know I should involve the
children more, but they do not understand my need for all
the socks to face the same direction in their drawers (is it
so wrong to take comfort in order?). I know I have to learn
to give things a superficial clean and tidy-up, but that's not
as easy as it sounds.

*   *   *

Rachel now thinks I have a gift because I snap-diagnosed
Deidre Duffy – one of the school mummies whom we
hardly know – as an alcoholic. It wasn't difficult. Deidre
stuck her head into our car at the two o'clock pick-up and
(a) she smelt of drink; (b) she talked too much and with
excessive, slow enthusiasm; (c) her face has puffed up
(*really* puffed up); and (d) Deidre's youngest child has been
at school for some years, yet Deidre still doesn't have a job.
At first, Rachel thought I was mad because (a) smelling of
drink doesn't make you an alcoholic – Deidre could have
had her lunch out with someone and had *one* glass of wine;
(b) perhaps Deidre is simply persistent and boring by
nature; (c) she could have put on weight for any one of
many reasons; and (d) I don't have a job either. But I said
Deidre had not had her lunch out with someone because

72

she was wearing a badly bobbled fleece and trainers, at which point Rachel started to sit up and listen and soon became convinced that I was right. (Of course I was right.) As I was driving her home, she said, in a Haley Joel Osment voice, 'Do you see dead people?' and, in a way, I sort of do.

* * *

Trevor has taken on the look of someone who's one of the dead people but just hasn't accepted it yet. Jill, on the other hand, looks marvellous. (Yah-boo to all those with pity in their hearts for her.)

* * *

We did what we always do on election day and brought the children with us to the polling station to witness democracy in action (my idea, obviously, and therefore my fault when they ran off/tried to pull the pencil off the string/mimed interfering with the boxes, etc.).

*

He is meeting Marilyn and Eddie Softly tonight, regarding Miss Morning's do, which is only a fortnight away. I am beginning to get a bad feeling about this function and wish some definite info would come home from school on the subject. Originally, I had thought this was going to be a big come-all-ye for the parents to mark the retirement of their beloved principal, but as time passes with no universal invitation, I'm starting to wonder.

*

I don't seem to see Rachel quite as much these days, which must mean she is using the other gate, or perhaps her children are going home from school on play-dates with other families. I'm not too concerned because when I do see her everything's still fine. But I hope it isn't because she said she'd help me put my house in order when she got back from her holidays and now finds she really doesn't want to – I'd rather keep her friendship and forget about the house, but I can't tell her how desperate I am to have a friend in case I scare her off.

* * *

Fuck. This is why I hate getting involved with other people. There *is* a guest list for this party, and I'm on it, and Rachel *isn't*, and the Duffys *aren't*, and the head boy's (quite glamorous) family *are*, but the head girl's (quite unglamorous and shy) family *aren't*, and the Dinsmores, whose four fat girls all went through Miss Morning's, *aren't*, and Marilyn's two sisters and their husbands, who have no connection whatsoever to the school, *are*. And then there are the 'plus ones', which seems to mean the single parents who are popular as individuals and whose estranged spouses are deemed not worth bothering about, so the single parents get to bring an additional adult of their choice. Like 'B. Wilson plus one', which is Brenda Wilson, who even *I* know moved her lover in before she'd moved her husband out, but Brenda is 'good fun'. 'R. McConville plus one' is the only single dad – I think he's the widower who owns the hire shop; he lends the school barbecues and bouncy castles for Fun Day free of charge. I asked my 'husband' about the kind-faced woman who is secretary of the Parents' Committee and does all the boring jobs like turning up early for events to turn on the tea-boilers and typing out the recipes for the Our Favourite Recipes book, which raised more than £2,000 for the nursery. He didn't think she was on the list. I love Miss Morning, but I hate this.

I am growing to hate this house, too. I have started wishing, again, that I lived in a wipe-clean box with only the essentials. The less we have, the less we would have to maintain. But while this is true, it denies the part of the problem that comes from within me, not without. The proportion of the problem that lies inside me is far, far bigger, I know. Bigger than everything else in my world. It has crazy dimensions that can collapse universes and eat them, like a black hole.

*

The votes won't be counted until Monday. Trevor is still suing everybody.

* * *

Today should have been a good day, even a great day, because Rachel and I are going to do our supermarket shopping together. I had stopped believing I would ever be such a person who goes supermarket shopping with her friend, and I know it's not unconnected to the facts of my having a large car boot and Rachel not having a car, but I don't think that's the *only* reason she suggested it, and even if it is, I don't care.

The one thing that is undermining my happiness at this turn of events, though, is the bloody surprise party. How can Marilyn not fail to see that this is not OK? I have been fretting all weekend about the injustices in the guest list, and the fact that there even *is* a guest list. (This is one of the reasons I'm so into voting: *everybody* is invited.)

I cannot see how I can go because of all the people who will wonder why they were overlooked. I know how that feels. Very bad. And you cannot ask for an explanation of your exclusion, so you tie yourself up in knots wondering why you fall short or whom you have offended. So I can't go. I can't be complicit in something that will engender that. But not going will seem like a slight – of Miss Morning or Marilyn, or both. So I could make an excuse, but that fails to stand up for my belief that exclusive gatherings hurt people. Again, I wonder, how can Marilyn not see that her plans are bound to wound, that this is not OK?

Even he has expressed misgivings. He thought it was going to be a party for everyone, too, until he saw the guest list. I have tried so hard for so long not to blunder, not to do irreparable damage (isn't that the only kind?). For so long I have lived my life in pencil, and now someone else has dictated that I must make a permanent mark, and I resent this and cannot concentrate on anything else for thinking about it.

*

Trevor got elected.

* * *

How humiliating. Yesterday after shopping we went into the supermarket café for a cup of tea. Shouting Barbara was there, as usual. She shouted over at Rachel, 'RACHEL! RACHEL! WHERE'S THE BABBIES T'DAY? WHERE'S THE BABBIES, T'DAY, RACHEL?'

Rachel called back, 'They're all at school, Barbara,' to which Barbara replied, 'OH, ARE THEY ALL AT SCHOOL? DO THEY LIKE SCHOOL, RACHEL?' Rachel wanted to look at the complimentary *Daily Mirror* and didn't really wish to be disturbed by Barbara, so she spread out the pages and made to read, while saying absently, 'Oh, they like it fine.' I never speak to anyone absently, not even the children. I couldn't. So I called out quite directly, 'What about you, Barbara, did you enjoy school?' and Barbara yelled across the entire café (across the entire supermarket, car park, town, planet and universe, it felt to me), 'DO YOU KNOW ME? RACHEL, WHO'S THAT GIRL WITH YOU WHO'S TALKING TO ME?'

How long have I lived in this town, shopped in this supermarket? How many times have I looked Shouting Barbara in the eye and greeted her unflinchingly while others ridiculed/pretended not to see her? Rachel, who has been here about five minutes, is deemed worthy of familiar chit-chat, while I am revealed as so far down the social pecking order that even Shouting Barbara hasn't registered my existence.

I am so invisible.

*

Rachel made me promise to shove the shopping away at speed, instead of doing all the lining up, labels forward, etc. I do not break promises, but I really don't see how it's a good idea in the long run to put new produce in front of old.

*

Meanwhile, I cannot believe my self-righteous ruminations of the past few days regarding Marilyn's party. Because that's what it is: Marilyn's party, which she is entitled to have for her friend and invite whomsoever she chooses. Who do I think I am?

* * *

Except: if it looks like a leaving do, and it sounds like a leaving do, mightn't people be forgiven for thinking it *is* a leaving do? So if Rachel or Deidre Duffy or the Parents' Committee woman asked me if I was at Miss Morning's leaving party, is there any way I could say, 'no' – unless I had actually stayed at home? Could I say, 'No, I wasn't at

Miss Morning's leaving party. However, I did attend Marilyn Softly's recent soirée, which coincided with Miss Morning's retirement and at which speeches were made and gifts presented in tribute to her and her career, but which wasn't actually her leaving do'? Unlikely, as their question and my answer would be taking place in *real life*.

For the first time, I slightly dread bumping into Rachel (along with the others whom I suspect will feel snubbed) in case news of the party has started leaching out. Plus, I am really struggling with my Core Tasks again, because I genuinely cannot concentrate for worrying about this bloody thing. Bloody, bloody Marilyn Softly. And she and her ringing voice are completely oblivious.

*

I couldn't put the tins in the cupboard the wrong way round. I tried, but I couldn't. That's not right, is it? But who/how could I ever ask for help with this? I cannot go to my GP, surely and say, 'I am unable to put my tins of food in the cupboard the wrong way round. Can you please prescribe a pill for this?' What's he going to give me? Something for tinnitus?

*

For now, I am going to take Diazepam for a couple of nights to get myself some sleep and break the cycle of anxiety. That's just being practical.

* * *

'Had we but world enough and time', I wouldn't spend it with a seventeenth-century sleazeball version of Woods.

*

Rachel thinks I am 'smart', and that this is a big part of the reason why I am busy all the time yet fail to achieve the results she does. For example, according to Rachel, she watches the DVDs of things, while I read the book; she throws all her household rubbish in one bin, which she parks at the kerb, while I sort everything and take it to the bottle bank/textiles bin/charity shop (Rachel didn't even know what I was doing when I took a window envelope and harvested from it the paper and used stamp); Rachel puts all charity appeals into the bin without opening them, while I feel duty-bound to read and contemplate each one, even if I have no money to donate, and recycle the paper they're printed on. Consequently, Rachel's domestic life shines, while mine is as it is. Does this *sound* smart?

By 'smart', I suspect Rachel means that I think about things which she doesn't, and doesn't expect to, and this much may be true. And she's right: it certainly doesn't get things done.

All this talk came about because Rachel appeared at school this morning ready to help me sort out my house. The timing couldn't have been better, because I felt wonderful after my Diazepam-ensured night's sleep. There's something energising about working in a team, and Rachel is so practical that we whisked through loads.

Of course, I began, as usual, to do things my way, but Rachel intervened, pointing out that if I spent an hour on one small putty mark on the window frame, I would only clean a single set of windows today, but, if I did as she told me, we'd get through most of the house. I did as she told me. For ten brilliant minutes, I followed Rachel round with a rubbish sack into which she emptied the kitchen and bathroom bins, before swiftly trawling the place, lifting biscuit wrappers, toilet-roll tubes, scrumpled-up felt-tip drawings and old tissues. I squirmed when Rachel dumped in entire newspapers (recycle! recycle!), but I kept it buttoned and Did As She Told Me. We filled a black sack in minutes. Rachel instructed me to tie it up and put it in the boot of the car.

Next, Rachel gathered up the dirty washing, including all the sheets and covers off the beds. She stuffed these in another black sack and is going to wash and dry them at her house because she has a tumble-dryer. (There's something uncomfortably intimate about this, but I am really trying to push my boundaries.)

From then on in, I saw that it was as much about what Rachel *doesn't* do as what she *does*. For example, Rachel doesn't package up all the mail addressed to this house's previous resident and take it to the post office for weighing and sending – she just throws it out; she doesn't wash the whole kitchen floor, she just wipes off the spills under the table and by the sink; she vacuums *round* furniture; she doesn't write lists. Rachel had another sharp-intake-of-breath moment when she opened the toy cupboard. She eventually said, 'What is it with you and cupboards?' and then turned all the boxes round the wrong way so you can't see the labels – *Large Vehicles, Small Vehicles, Construction/Fire, Airport/Space, Dressing Up, Lego, Action Figures, Suitable for under-3s, Odds and Ends*, etc. – and just heeled the toys into any old boxes and closed the doors.

As we were having our tea break, the best thing of all happened. Rachel asked me again about the rally, and I told her a bit about where it is and what it is and why it is, and I think we might actually go!

I also told Rachel about Pete and the vibrator, and we listened for it for a little while (to no avail). I am not a natural gossip and felt a bit tawdry, but I think if I want to keep this friendship I need to act more like other people. Anyway, Americans call it 'sharing'.

I hardly thought at all about the Miss Morning party situation. Rachel didn't mention it, which presumably means she hasn't heard anything. I am going to take my Diazepam for one more night, to consolidate my gains, but then I will stop. (Diazepam is highly addictive.)

* * *

No Rachel at the gate today, so I'm back to shopping on my own. I noticed that I am the sort of person who manages to say, 'Thanks' and 'Bye' so many times in the process of leaving the supermarket check-out that it embarrasses both me and the otherwise unmovable cashier. 'Thanks,' I say, as I load the groceries into bags. 'Thanks,' I say, as she packs a few to hasten me. 'Thanks,' I say, again as I hand her my plastic card, and 'Thanks,' I repeat, as she provides the means to verify it. 'Thanks,' I say again, when I offer back the verifying information. 'Thanks,' I reiterate, as she hands me my card and receipts. 'Thanks,' I say, as she pushes the last of the bags further down the slope towards me, and 'Thanks. 'Bye . . . ', as I file the card and dockets into my purse. 'Thanks. 'Bye . . . ', I repeat, as I load the last of the bags into the trolley. 'Thanks. Bye . . . ', finally, as I swing round the trolley and depart. And all with an artificial smile.

*

Why is everyone suddenly referring to Miss Morning as *Jane* Morning. Her first name *is* Jane, but no one used it before – until now, it was always *Miss* Morning. Is it because we're almost at the end of something (the school year, Miss Morning's career)? Is it like that last-day-of-term thing, when you still came to school but you could wear your own clothes and bring in games and the teacher didn't wear a tie?

*

I will never be the girl in the song. Not any song. Not ever. Unless there's some lean, long-haired young singer-songwriter out there who eschews gorgeous chiseled-featured slinky creatures in favour of . . . what? Even I can't describe me. I am pretty confident no one has ever tossed and turned in their bed at night yearning for me, and if they didn't do it when I was seventeen and had cascading hair and reasonable teeth, they're certainly not going to do it now.

*

I am determined to stick with Rachel's dynamic housekeeping ways. No more lists, no more hand-carved strategies. 'Doing it is doing it.'

*

The smell in our car is back with a vengeance, but at least this time I know what it is. I must drop off that black bag at the dump.

*

Last night, I had that hateful thing where you're asleep but you can't breathe, and you know you're asleep, and you feel that if you can't get a proper breath in, you'll suffocate before you can waken up and save yourself. I think it's probably psychological.

* * *

Well, well, well. The Blessed Eleanor came visiting today, and got the shock of her life. No crumb-and-crisps-strewn hallway to greet her; instead, I brought her through to the kitchen, where Rachel sat in shorts and a vest, drinking her cup of tea. Eleanor took in the scene: cleanliness, order, the folded dishcloth draped over the mixer tap. It clearly unnerved her. For an alarming split second, I saw it enter her mind that I had hired a domestic cleaner and that Rachel was her, so I leaped in and explained that Rachel is *my friend* and, to Rachel, that Eleanor is my mother.

So, which was the greatest moment in a day of great moments? Was it when Rachel stuck out her hand to greet Eleanor and offered her a cup of tea? (Yes, Mother, I have a real friend who feels so at home in *my* home that she can propose beverages.) Or was it when Eleanor said she would 'do the boys' rooms', and Rachel and I exchanged a glance before I told my mother (for the first time ever) that the job was already done. Or perhaps it was when, as I knew she would, Eleanor tried to undermine this new alliance by saying, 'And has she got you using all these natural products, Rachel?' (because I won't use bleach or any other household cleaner with big black Xs on the label and which requires protective clothing and breathing apparatus and *Rachel backed me up.*

Obviously, my mother awarded all credit for my improved domestic situation to Rachel, but, by association, because *I* have engaged Rachel's friendship, some of this credit sneaks back to me.

* * *

The trouble with 'sharing' is once you start, you can't stop. I bumped into the kind-faced woman from the Parents'

Committee while crossing the school playground this morning, and she asked me if my 'husband' would make a little gift presentation at Miss Morning's party on behalf of the committee. Officially, Caroline (as I now know her to be called) doesn't even know about the function but, in fact, she has endured a mutually cringing exchange with someone who *is* invited and who assumed that Caroline was too (exactly the kind of thing I have been worrying about), and so, unofficially, she knows quite well. When, Caroline's composure faltered, as she explained this to me, I blurted out (and I am not a blurter) how uncomfortable I felt about the whole thing and how even *he* now regrets getting involved in something so unexpectedly exclusive but is now in too deep to withdraw. I even 'shared' my info about the sisters and brothers-in-law who would be attending, which, I fear, made matters worse. Marilyn Softly was on playground duty some yards away, and I felt she must know what we were discussing, but I couldn't curtail the conversation and walk away because then Caroline would have felt that absolutely everyone had turned their backs on her. She sees it as a Staff v. Parents' Committee scenario, in which the staff have happily taken the thousands of pounds she has raised and the hundreds of hours she has volunteered, and then, when it's time to party, none of them has said, 'What about Caroline? We insist she be included.'

*

Miss Morning's brother is coming round to our house this evening to contribute facts to the *This Is Your Life*-type speech. He is a busy police inspector and will not hang about, I think. I will take the children out for a drive and an ice cream.

(The house is tidy! Someone is coming round and I am not afraid!)

*

Half way through my conversation with Caroline, I realised that we were directly under the window of the vice-principal's office. Although I had said nothing untrue, I had been, by my standards, indiscreet. I probably became a little bit careful of what I said from that moment on, but I didn't change my line completely because I couldn't be so dishonest. I'm worried. I believe the vice-principal to be discreet himself, and possibly noble. But I don't know who else may have been in that office.

* * *

Should I approach Marilyn face to face and explain the concerns that are rattling round my head? She could still call off the party, and no harm would have been done. Marilyn is happily ignorant of the furore about to be unleashed. That is, if there *is* a furore about to be unleashed. If there *isn't*, and I express my concerns to Marilyn, then all I will have done is needlessly spoil a perfectly nice occasion. But is there any way this function can go ahead and *not* upset lots of people? If I were Marilyn, would I want me to tell me what I am thinking?

Meanwhile, Rachel and I have gone ahead and booked the coach seats for the anti-poverty rally, but I cannot enjoy even this, in the circumstances.

*

I need to concentrate to track down accommodation for Friday and Saturday nights, which I (somewhat recklessly) promised Rachel I could do, and I *can't* concentrate because of worries about fallout from this party.

*

Caroline has decided against sending a gift for presentation at a party to which she is not invited. She will arrange to hand it over some other way.

*

I am not going to feel bad about making a list of stuff to be packed for this trip. Sometimes lists are appropriate.

*

There are no family rooms! I cannot find one in the entire city. And we need two.

*   *   *

As he shaved and dressed for Miss Morning's party, I felt a substantial twinge of regret that I will not be there. As Caroline pointed out, now that there will have been one leaving do, even if undeclared, there will not be another. So, I've missed my chance to be part of the only farewell to a woman who mattered to me. Me and my big conscience. However, I can still tap into comforting feelings of solidarity with the plebeian parents who seemingly didn't matter enough to be included (if not quite the Wretched of the Earth, then possibly the Wretched of the Parking Bay). There is Caroline, for example, and Deidre Duffy, and the head girl's family and the other 'little' people whose names nobody seems to know. And Rachel – how could I have looked her in the eye had I socialised with the 'in crowd' while she was not deemed important enough to be told about their party, much less invited?

*

After six hours on the Internet, I have found two triple rooms plus a fold-up bed in an ungraded guest house. That's OK. We're going there to put a stop to poverty, not for a spa weekend.

* * *

He had a really good night. His speech went very well, and everyone enjoyed themselves. The only blight on proceedings was a very angry announcement made by a very angry Marilyn before the arrival of the VIP (Miss Morning). According to him, Marilyn stood up at the top table and said that Someone had been pronouncing on who should and shouldn't have been included in this party, and that she was livid and would scratch out the eyes of Whoever it was when she found Them out, and that this was her private family party, and had always been her private family party, and that she had invited people whom she thought would get along, and who would also get along with Miss Morning, with the aim of having a good night's fun.

The R. McConville on the guest list was Rachel. When he told me this, I thought I would vomit. Then I thought I would fall down. How stupid that I never even thought of Rachel having a second name. I remembered that the hire-shop widower is actually called Robert McCanvey. He wasn't there.

*

How can I enjoy going on the coach, this evening, in these circumstances?

*

Stephen the computer guy is coming round this afternoon to defragment our computer. I wish he could do the same for my head.

* * *

All my anxieties have flown away, and I find I am in my element. Somewhat (but not completely) to my surprise, Rachel hasn't really travelled at all. She has been on a coach to Blackpool, but apart from that, she's just flown between airports and taken flexibuses to resorts. So now *I* am the expert.

*

Wow! Rachel really *isn't* a traveller, though her kids are taking to it just fine. She can't read a map and keeps wanting to go into cafés for mochaccinos, which will blow our budget to pieces. Admittedly, the guest house is pretty grim, but the kettle and cups look perfectly clean (even if you could get Legionnaire's disease from the shower curtain), and that's how you have your cuppas free.

*

Today has been the best day for a very long time. I do not care about small-town soireés and small-minded exclusivity. And I am proud of my ever-recycled spectacles (I packed the Sellotape). This is where I want to be: rallying with people of conscience, making placards and banners and taking penalty shots against a man in a George W. Bush mask, dancing barefoot on the grass with my children to the African musicians on the giant screen. Our children dragged Rachel's into a row and copied the elderly woman in front of them who was quietly practising her t'ai chi. They did it like line-dancing, and even strangers walking by were laughing at them. I am energised by this atmosphere of Together We Are Strong. I am Leaping Water. I am Falling Rain. I am Light on the Mountain. I am not inside out today, and I have not felt tired once.

*

How can Rachel not have figured out Steve? As we set off for home (our guest house), he appeared from a facing street – fortyish, hailing us, wanting our help. He was trying to find the flexibus to his campsite so he could join his wife and children who had gone on ahead. It was small wonder he was having difficulty getting a signal on his mobile, I reckoned, because there is a low, shaded dip, just at that part of the road, with tall trees on one side and tenements on two others. He was holding it out the way long-sighted people hold menus, trying to find the optimum distance for him to focus. Steve told us his name, and we told him ours. It was that kind of day. He and his family hadn't managed to walk the route at all, because the rally had been massively bigger than expected. This was his first such rally, he said, and asked if it was ours. He was there because he tried, in his way, to be a good Christian – how about us? He was such a liar!

'Steve' was an undercover cop. When I observed this to Rachel, after he'd gone, she thought at first that I was joking, and then that I had an overactive imagination, but soon it was the Deidre Duffy thing all over again. I mean, I asked her: (1) Have you ever seen anyone who has been camping the night before? They don't look like a freshly bathed baby, like Steve did. (2) Yes, he had a bit of stubble, but it was (a) very slight and (b) completely out of step with the rest of him. (3) What kind of haircut was that? The kind of short-but-not-policeman-short haircut that only a policeman who is pretending not to be a policeman would go for. (4) Who uses your name five or six times, having just met you, unless they are (a) trying to memorise it (why? Steve was never going to see us again) or (b) speaking for the benefit of someone or something else (like a concealed microphone)? (5) If he was genuinely looking for his flexibus stop, why didn't he ask any of the dozen policemen who were within shouting distance, as I eventually did on his behalf, while he hung strangely back (knowing they would recognise him as 'one of their own')? (6) Miles from home, a nice guy like him leaves his wife single-handed to marshal the children to their out-of-town campsite? I don't think so. He gave us big hugs at the end, and there may have been sincerity in that, and in the 'Christian' remark, or he may have been checking us for something else. I didn't get the final thing until later, when Rachel took out her mobile, and I thought to ask her if it takes pictures. She showed me how, holding it out like she was long-sighted and it was a menu.

* * *

I am so happy (though also so wound up). I am starting to see where I really belong. I am going to join Amnesty International *and* Greenpeace *and* Friends of the Earth. And Rachel and I are probably going to get our noses pierced. It's taken a long time, but perhaps, finally, I am getting to get to grips with who I really am. I will look back on this weekend as the time when my life restarted. I am going to have adventures again, and this time I have Rachel to share in them.

*

Rachel and I talked and talked on the coach home. The thing is, Rachel doesn't judge me. She knows what I'm like and just accepts me. I think she also values my insight into what's going on below the surface of people – that is, certain people: set me in front of a truly healthy specimen and I'm stumped, but bring out your addicts, your compulsives, your 'dead', and I'll give you chapter and verse.

Oh, and, yes: some of the others on the coach said that after we had disembarked one stop early yesterday (so Rachel could get her first gourmet coffee), a police photographer boarded and made everybody have their picture taken. So I was definitely right about Steve – but had he been following us, believing us to be subversives who were deliberately evading recognition? We didn't know about the photographer, we were just seeking refreshment. Big Brother or what?

*

I do wish the choking dreams would stop. They come when I lie on my back, so I am reduced to sleeping in a bra filled with tennis balls, worn over my shoulder blades. I'm not actually afraid to fall asleep, but I *nearly* am.

* * *

A terrible thing has happened. I was speaking to the head girl's shy mother at the school gate. They have just come back from a fortnight in Portugal (they got great weather), so *they weren't overlooked for Miss Morning's party, as I rumour-mongered. They were away.* As she told me quietly of what a lovely time they had had, I became acutely aware of Marilyn Softly standing within earshot. Suddenly, she seemed icily silent and, even with her eyes facing forward, ever so watchful. My blood rises again to my ears, just thinking about it. I feel sick. I was wrong. This is too, too bad. I am poisoned with shame.

*   *   *

Rachel is leaving! Rachel is moving back where she came from to set up home with her boyfriend (what *boyfriend?) With whom she went on holiday to Spain! With whom she attended Miss Morning's leaving do! Our trip to the anti-poverty rally was, in effect, her bloody hen night in Bohemia, her last 'wild' act to show herself and her boyfriend that she could still be a free spirit! And how do I know all this? Not from Rachel, with whom I have just spent the weekend, but from Marilyn Softly (who else) who knows everything about all our movements, because all our children go to her school.*

    Rachel is leaving.

*

Am I wrong about *everything*? I went next door to Stephanie on the pretext of getting the boiler-service man's phone number (but actually because I was getting a bad, choking feeling in my throat which made me afraid of being in the house on my own). I was lucky to catch her, as she was on her way out to salsacise class with Jill at the leisure centre. As soon as I crossed the threshold, I thought I would fall down on the spot because I could hear the now-familiar whirring of their vibrator, and Stephanie was leading me towards it. It was one of those surreal moments when you wonder if you are awake or having a nightmare. I desperately looked for means to stall, but I had no laces to pretend to tie, and there was no artwork on the walls that I could stop to admire, and the noise was coming nearer, and I thought, again, that I would either vomit or fall down, and wished, wished, wished that this was a dream, and felt a little bit like I was going mad, until, in front of us, Pete appeared from the kitchen, smiling in a Friends of the Earth T-shirt and *rotating the handle on a wind-up radio.*

I may laugh about this at some point in the future.

*

What does she mean? What the fuck does Rachel mean? She has just accused me of being some kind of addict. I screwed up my courage and phoned her to ask why she is leaving, and why she didn't tell me, and I suppose I was having a slight go at her, but she really went for me. She took all the stuff I explained to her about alcoholics and their good days and bad days and how they are terrible liars and deluded but crafty and how the drink always has to be looked after first, etc., etc. – but we were talking about her uncle Nigel – and she turned it round on me. The scary thing is, I can sort of see where she's coming from.

I sort of fit. 'I don't know what you're on, but for your own sake,' she said, although it didn't feel like it was for my sake, 'stop pretending and get it sorted. If you won't do it for yourself, do it for your kids.' What am I on? I'm not on anything, am I? Something is really, truly wrong here.

*

I feel utterly betrayed. I tried phoning Rachel again. I thought I was getting somewhere until she said, 'Well, Eleanor says . . . '. Well, Eleanor says a great deal. I always knew that if I introduced any two of my friends or acquaintances they would quickly like each other better than either of them liked me. I just hadn't figured on it extending to my family. Rachel has been discussing me with Eleanor. She has told her about finding my Notes for the Next Time. And I cannot bear it.

*

Has Rachel uncovered the real reason why I haven't achieved Sebastian the rocking-horse or the piano or the cuckoo clock? Is it the same reason that Woods and Wendy treat me like something brittle, why Jill and Stephanie do things together and I am left on the outside, why I have put on this weight, why I have broken glasses, no clothes and no job and where adventures only lie locked in the past? I thought domestic life would be like a Doris Day musical. Instead, it is the postal backlog and the inability to clean my own house and this.

*

I have had enough of blinking and squirming and gasping.

Perhaps I *should* make exercise a priority. It's supposed to be a great stress-buster.

De-fragment.

Green tea is meant to be good.

Help. Help me.

* * *

I am stranded. I am so far out on this limb that I cannot get back. If I move, the bough will break. If I don't move, I will fall, fall, fall.

*

Oh, God, no. I can hear the window-cleaners. This is the worst, because if I ignore their ring they will come on anyway. With their ladders and buckets they will swarm the house. Upstairs and down. I want to hide, but there is no hiding-place, and the worst exposure of all is not simply to be found but to be found while hiding.

I cower like a kitten in a cage. The hands are coming in for me.

*

Sometimes, Diazepam just isn't enough.

Angels

He and I got on quite well there, for a day. We actually laughed, although it was probably nervous laughter, as we were on our way to his vasectomy clinic. We stopped at the garage shop for petrol, and I went inside to buy him a bar of chocolate. When I buy him chocolate, I have to make sure it's something we both know I don't like, otherwise it looks suspiciously as though I've really bought it for myself. So I bought him Cadbury's Whole Nut. Whoops.

(In the car, he confided in me what he's been hearing about Woods. (Woods hasn't been round for quite a while. Everybody knows he doesn't like to be near people with problems.) Seemingly, Woods asked Wendy if they could go on holiday to Tenerife with their daughter, Billie and Wendy told him to get lost and said he couldn't play Happy Families for the duration of one holiday and dump them again as soon as they hit the tarmac. So Woods went to Tenerife by himself and then started ringing Wendy saying that when he returned he wanted to try again, but when he actually got back, he acted like those phone conversations had never happened. No wonder Wendy is as hard and cool as she is. She has had to toughen up to survive. Anyway, I was surprised to hear myself encourage him to have a night out with Woods, just in case Woods really is screwed up and needs someone to talk to. I very much doubt he pours his heart out to his lady friends. (Needless to say, Woods's father was an alcoholic.))

So this was my first time inside a private hospital. Blimey. Instead of a grumpy clerk in a pinafore, we were greeted by a sleek sixty-something hostess. She settled us into the empty waiting area, which had no wipe-clean vinyl seating or old copies of *Chat* magazine and actually looked more like the residents' lounge of a select hotel. I felt I should be ordering a gin and tonic. A smiling nurse came and ushered us into a sweet little carpeted lift with brass fittings and then swished us along corridors to his ward. Of course, at every set of fire-doors, I expected to leave the carpet behind and, as National Health refugees, cross a threshold into Eastern Bloc austerity, but it didn't happen. He was shown into a private en-suite room, where he lay watching *Grandstand* all day, while they mucked up his medication, so we came home intact.

Eleanor had graciously looked after the children at her bungalow. I don't know if she guessed what we were doing.

I had simply said he required a minor procedure and wouldn't be able to drive after the anaesthetic. When we called to collect our offspring, she gave me a little report on the day's events, in a tone that implied, 'I don't know why you make such a meal of it – looking after a few children is hardly arduous.' But Eleanor gave them chicken nuggets and microwave chips and let them lie on the floor playing PlayStation and watching DVDs for eight hours. She wasn't comparing like with like.

*

Having got on so well – first with the laughing and then with me looking after him when they messed up his usual medication – I knew he would expect this to translate into sex, which it didn't, and that the air would then blacken again, which it did.

*

There is a new t'ai chi class starting at the further education college. It is at tea time on Wednesdays, so there's really no good reason why he couldn't look after the children and let me go. I don't precisely know what t'ai chi is, but it appears calming.

*

People can remark on your 'infectious laugh' all your life, but it still won't feature in your obituary should you die of something contagious.

*

Are apes, in actual fact, good mimics?

*

Django Reinhardt playing 'Autumn Leaves' is on the radio. You don't hear that every day. Despite its poignant beauty, I cannot get past thinking that our garden paths are still blocked by *last* year's autumn leaves and already they are falling again.

I don't have the teeth for a grand affair in later life.

*

He said, angrily, 'I don't think you know what you want.' And, in a way, he's right. I don't. When you-know-who went away, I thought she had split me right open with her scalpel words and my mind and my guts were all on view. But, it turns out, she didn't say enough. I am now reconciled to, and even grateful for, the insight that I am some sort of addict but, weirdly, I do not yet know what I am addicted to. So I want to be free, but don't yet know free of what.

Sometimes the first bit of insight isn't enough.

*

Like Samuel Beckett, I have only one certainty beyond the knowledge that I was born, live and will die, which is the knowledge that I can't shut up. (At least, not for long.)

*

Jill was out on her bike, today. She even looks good in a cycling helmet.

* * *

Pete and Stephanie are moving house. It was quite a shock to see the for-sale board when we drove home from shopping. In a fit of irritation about something else, I wickedly told the children it was because of their unbearable noise that Pete and Stephanie and their well-behaved girls are leaving. It was wrong to say it, although it's probably partly true.

*

I have posted my form for t'ai chi.

* * *

Down the garden at the washing line this morning, I thought, Does a fly ever look at a dewy spider's web and see a thing of beauty instead of a trap? Or is that only we humans?

* * *

Stephanie told me over the wall today that they might not be moving. Pete is fed up trying to keep ahead of the big garden, that's all, so they thought they'd put the sale board up and see what the interest was; if there isn't much response, they'll just stay where they are. Since arriving at our place, we have visibly killed the once beautiful garden with neglect, so Stephanie's reference touched a nerve, which I tried to defend with jocularity. Stephanie just looked at me.

Obviously, living in the identical-twin house to theirs, I am more than a little curious about the asking price.

*

105

People say, 'if you want something done, ask a busy person.' But do they ever consider the reasons why busy people are busy? I mean, look at it this way: you *don't* hear people say, 'if you want your drinks cabinet cleared out and tidied, ask an alcoholic.' (By 'drinks cabinet', I mean top shelf of the larder, obviously. By 'larder' I mean the big formica cupboard in the kitchen.) But can people be addicted to being busy? Am *I*?

* * *

Pete and Stephanie's house is in the paper today, but it's with the estate agency that doesn't print the prices. It does, however, have a website, which I may peruse.

*

I felt like I was poking through someone's bins, and I also felt as though Pete and Stephanie could see me as I hunted down the info about their house. However, the price was quite impressive. Of course, there's no guarantee that people will get their asking price. Sometimes houses stay on the market for months and seem to become unsellable, and everybody always surmises that it's because the vendors are asking for too much money. (Why do 'people' suddenly become 'vendors' when they are selling houses (or ice cream)?)

*

Here comes another weekend.

* * *

Confirmation of my registration for t'ai chi came today. I wonder how many will be in the class. I am *not* thinking about making a new friend. The whole thing with you-know-who has set me back on that front. I saw a dark-haired girl pushing a buggy near the roundabout at the weekend and, oh, just for a second . . .

* * *

There is a constant stream of callers at Pete and Stephanie's. It must be exhausting trying to keep the place tidy. I think we can safely say there is a great deal of interest.

*

I should have bought a new T-shirt for t'ai chi tomorrow.

* * *

Could things have been any worse? First, who turned up at t'ai chi tonight but Marilyn Softly. She called out a hello, but there was a metallic edge to her ringing voice. She wasn't expecting me, either. Second, there was Philomena. Philomena is the t'ai chi teacher, and she is built like the proverbial brick shit-house. (Proverbial? How would that proverb go, then? 'People who live in brick shit-houses . . . can throw whatever they like'?) Having introduced herself in a speech straight from an adult learners' training manual, Philomena taught us to do a sunrise movement, which I quite liked, before getting into the big topic of the night, which was Getting *Grounded.* Apparently it's all to do with putting down these imaginary roots from the soles of your feet, and it's really, really important in life as well as in t'ai chi class. Philomena gave us an example from her personal experience (Adult Learners' Training Manual, Lesson 2 – use personal anecdotes) of a crowd of youths coming running up behind her and then parting like the Red Sea and going *round* her because she had heard them advancing, *grounded* herself and deflected their energy. In order to demonstrate the power of being grounded, Philomena got into her stance with her feet shoulder-width apart and then invited someone to try to dislodge her. Except she didn't invite just someone. She invited me. She invited me because, in the space of thirty silent minutes in a room of fifteen candidates, I was the most screamingly feeble, ungrounded person alive. She was right. I couldn't shift her, and I couldn't even try properly because she looked so solid that I felt I would have needed a sharp stick. At Philomena's insistence, we then swapped roles. I was to stand as I normally do, which, because I am honest, meant folding my arms and putting all my weight on one leg. One good nudge and I was practically on my arse. Philomena also told us that we all swing like pendulums in our daily life, sometimes bouncing far too fast and high from side to side, and sometimes having almost no momentum; t'ai chi is going to get us swinging just the right amount all the time. I felt like swinging a large pendulum right between Philomena's eyes. For the first time since I was about six years old, I really wanted to kick a person up the bum.

At least Marilyn Softly being there meant something productive came of it. She owes me some bad karma after I boycotted her party, and my humiliation in her presence gets me closer to a clean slate. (But that's all a bit Notes for the Next Time, isn't it? And I'm supposed to be steering away from that.)

* * *

He is going out with Woods tonight. Suits me – I have taped a two-part crime drama and can watch both episodes back to back (although I dare say I've already seen the best bits in the trailers).

* * *

He came in at nearly five, after quite a night of it. Fuelled by Bacardi Breezers, four of them climbed over the fence at the golf-and-ski centre and had wheelie-bin races down the dry slope before retiring to Woods's for further refreshment and Rod Stewart karaoke. By five o'clock, he was past being sick, and I have to admit I admire his ability to get up and go to work the next day.

I was surprised, and yet also not surprised, to hear that Woods had had a minor fling with you-know-who. Or perhaps it was just a one-night stand. Something, anyway.

* * *

How is it that both my parents deny they have split up yet each has a separate explanation for why they have parted? Terry, my father, the oldest beatnik in town, claims it is because Eleanor completely refused to learn to speak Italian with him even though he really wanted her to. Eleanor says it is because she could no longer live with my father's addiction to purchasing buy-one-get-one-frees. (My parents couldn't just have sexual incompatibility or 'grow apart', like anyone else.) So now Eleanor is living alone in their bungalow (although all summer Terry still tended *and ate* his tomatoes in the greenhouse there), and he is staying in the little beach flatlet, into which he has crammed a second freezer to accommodate his special offers.

Is it any wonder I am the way I am?

* * *

Today, I had my first visit from Prentiss Prine, sent to me by the Listening Angels Trust. The Trust is a charity set up by a woman whose daughter killed herself because she had no one to talk to. That's the short version anyway. So now a team of Listening Angels is at large making sure troubled people have someone to 'share' with. The Angels aren't volunteers – they get paid £6.59 an hour and 60p a mile for petrol. (I've seen their recruitment ad in the paper.) I was assigned an Angel due to my episode at the start of the summer, and it's OK that the house is rough and malodorous because we both know she wouldn't be here if I wasn't dysfunctional.

Prentiss Prine is an American. I forget from which part. She came over here to research her family tree and to write a book, and she works as an Angel part-time. She has been here three years and has an on-off relationship with a man called Seamus Kelly whom she met here; she doesn't know how long she will stay. Prentiss has a brother in rehab and a sister with an eating disorder and she, Prentiss, gives thanks every day that in so troubled a family she, Prentiss, has managed to come through so healthy and unscathed. (Have you ever heard of anyone being 'scathed', by the way?) She was very excited to hear that I had joined a t'ai chi class, as she studied t'ai chi for six years with one of the top teachers in the States. She asked me about a lot of moves that I'd never heard of, but she seemed to enjoy talking about, and she's going to bring me some incense next week, which she says is the best kind of incense for t'ai chi. Prentiss is concerned about the cost to her teeth of living this side of the Atlantic. Seemingly, dentistry in the USA is different from what's on offer here. She also suggested I get a new pair of glasses like hers, which she really likes, and asked me if I would wish her to accompany me on a spa day or even to the hairdresser's, seeming to be under the impression that I am (a) rich, and (b) agoraphobic.

Prentiss Prine wears cowboy boots with jeans and a hippie top and seemed to me to be more of a Talking Angel.

* * *

Woods is coming under pressure from his new girlfriend who wants to move in with him. Woods is saying no, because his new girlfriend has a child about the same age as Billie, and how could he choose not to live with Billie and live with this other child instead? Also, I say 'his new girlfriend', but actually mean 'one of his new girlfriends' – her living *in situ* would also be pretty hard to explain to the other one.

* * *

I farted at t'ai chi, last night. I think I sort of over-relaxed. I can't go back. I'm going to have to learn it from a book instead. (Or maybe Prentiss could teach me. If I can ever get a word in edgeways to ask her.)

* * *

In my efforts to go cold turkey on my apparent need for maniacally busy activity, I have lately tried to approach housework like an acting role. I imagine I am auditioning to play a character who is superficial about housekeeping so I vaguely lift the debris from the surfaces of rooms, run the Hoover lightly over them, swish a microfibre cloth across visibly dusty places, that kind of thing. He has remarked on the difference, so it must be working a bit, but just skimming the whole house daily is tediously boring. I have to wonder if I was, indeed, getting some kind of gratification from trying to tackle the impossible housekeeping challenges of the past. Today I couldn't resist a little dejunking and went through everyone's wardrobes for finished-with summer clothes, which I took to the Listening Angels' charity shop. Ironically, I couldn't get chatting with the woman operating the till as her hearing-aid battery was on the blink. There was no reason for this to deter Shouting Barbara, however, who seems to shuttle endlessly between the supermarket café and the charity shops and who pounced on my bags as I carried them in from the car. As if I would have anything to fit Shouting Barbara! I may have put on a bit of weight, but nothing like that! I behaved as though I had never seen her in my life before, since she snubbed me that last time. I slightly wanted to teach her a lesson but do not think I succeeded in the least.

* * *

My new approach to housework may create a slightly tidier impression of our home, but it does not solve everything. Next week, I will have to audition for the role of someone who will efficiently cull their mountainous postal backlog in one week.

*

Trevor was in the paper *again*. (This town's answer to Jude Law.) This time, he was apparently pointing to no thirty m.p.h. speed limit on the road past the primary school near Woods's apartment. Looks like Trevor is managing OK as an independent.

* * *

Pete and Stephanie have sold their house. Already! The notice was across the sale board when I was doing the school run this morning. My best hope is that they have sold to deaf, liberal Bohemians who will become my friends and love me and my children exactly as we are. My worst fear is that they will have sold to anally retentive disciplinarians who will be horrified by the foul-mouthed brats, the rampant dandelions and my screeching.

*

Although I suspect she is verging on insane, I find myself looking forward to Prentiss's visit, tomorrow.

* * *

Prentiss Prine has a child! An eight-year-old boy called Ben, who lives with his father in the States. Prentiss felt it would have been unfair to uproot him and bring him over here with her. She also felt that boys and their fathers have a special bond, which ideally should not be broken. It turns out I am a sexist bigot, because I felt that, as Ben's mummy (or *mommy*), Prentiss should ideally have remained at the very least in the same (large) country as her son. Of course, I didn't say this. How, with her sense of entitlement to do what she wants, will Prentiss ever be able to relate to *me*?

Prentiss is also learning reiki healing massage. She is going to carry out a practice session on me next week as part of her coursework. I hope she knows what she's doing. I really cannot afford to have my energies any more misdirected than they already are.

*

114

At the school gate today, someone asked me how you-know-who was getting on, and then a few other people joined in. They obviously don't know about our schism. But I felt a certain rise in status because of all these people thinking of you-know-who as especially *my* friend, which more than balanced out the mild embarrassment of saying that I hadn't been in touch just recently. What on earth would you-know-who have made of Prentiss?

I wonder what Prentiss's house is like.

I wonder what Rachel's new place is like. Rachel. It's OK. I can say it. I can say 'Rachel' and it's OK.

*

Right. I am giving myself until Hallowe'en to get all excess detritus cleared out of this house. Then I will be able to enjoy the run-up to my beloved Christmas surrounded by a sense of order.

* * *

I have decided to open up to Prentiss Prine. I am going to tell her everything. I am going to tell her about the clutter and the busyness and the biscuit tins and Rachel and the Notes for the Next Time and Eleanor and Terry and him and *everything*. She might be mad, but she's all I've got.

* * *

I got really ruthless with the postal backlog today. I threw out all the back issues of letters from St Dunstan's and Ethiopiaid, etc. If I haven't got the money to help blind ex-

115

servicemen right now, it's not helping them see any better because I have a dozen of their newsletters in a carrier bag on the kitchen bench. I am also starting to feel slightly resentful of the foot-and-mouth painters, who keep sending us more and more notelets, presumably because we are among the elite who made the mistake of buying their calendar. This is where he and I differ: I do not like any of the foot-and-mouth paintings, and therefore do not wish to buy still more of their efforts. He does not wish to buy them either (because how many flowery notelets can one man use?) yet he thinks the paintings are really good *because he takes into consideration that they were done by someone holding their brush between their toes.* How did we ever get together?

* * *

At Prentiss's suggestion, I called into the Angels' charity shop again today, this time to offer my services as a volunteer. Prentiss does seem to think I need coaxing to get out into the community. The hearing-aid lady was on duty again (Trevor should be pictured with her in the paper, pointing at no batteries), which made communication arduous. Eventually, she got me to write down my name, address and telephone number to pass on to her boss. I hadn't realised I had to clear a selection process, but if they want a CV, I've got plenty of experience of hanging up other people's unloved clothing in dingy surroundings.

*

Terry called to see the children today. He brought them a paper bag of late tomatoes. They don't like tomatoes, so he ate them himself and taught them to play bridge (in Italian). Sometimes I just want to lie down on the floor and laugh.

Sometimes I just want to lie down on the floor and cry.

* * *

I have joined the Parents' Committee at school. I have done it for all the wrong reasons. The right reasons, presumably, would be a desire to support the teaching professionals by raising extra revenue through beetle drives and Christmas fairs, etc. My reasons were: (1) kind-faced Caroline stopped me in the playground and asked me to attend the meeting and I felt obliged and (2) I wanted to have something to put on my resumé for the Angels' shop volunteer post. So now, somehow, I have managed to become Honorary Assistant Secretary of the Parents' Committee. It shouldn't be too bad, as I am a fast typist. It was actually Marilyn Softly, the committee's staff liaison, who nominated me for the position. She put a sly little glint in her eye as she smiled at me, just to let me know this was another form of revenge, but as I had my own reasons for accepting, I didn't even attempt to fight back. Caroline is still the secretary, because nobody came forward to relieve her, and the meeting mostly consisted of people making it clear what they weren't prepared to do. Lots of people weren't prepared to approach local businesses for raffle prizes after last term, when a gas barbecue and a case of wine went missing from the PE store. Other people weren't prepared to do any more fund-raising but wanted instead to get the two o'clock parking mayhem sorted out. I said I wasn't prepared to be left in sole charge of the tea-boilers when we were doing hospitality for school functions (I do not understand them), and everybody laughed, even Marilyn, but I don't know if they laughed because they absolutely shared my tea-boiler anxiety or because I had (again, again) said something inappropriate. Anyhow, I am now in charge of the red book in which those attending meetings write their names, and I am going to attempt to put all their contact details into my e-mail, which will take me some time. I am not trying to be perfect, but I am trying to get on top of the situation from the start.

* * *

Prentiss used her listening hour to give me a reiki massage on the sofa. Shouldn't she have given me the £6.59 worth of listening first, and then done the reiki (*her coursework*) in her own time? However, I did feel something ebbing away from me under that blanket, and when Prentiss left, I cried.

* * *

I have slowly but successfully managed to put all of the Parents' Committee's contact details into my e-mail. My entire e-mail contacts list is now: eight people on the Parents' Committee, Rachel and Eleanor. How sad.

* * *

Margaret, the Angels' charity-shop manager, phoned to chat about me joining her team. She asked if I had any retail experience, and I was able to say I had, although it was a long time ago. (There weren't many jobs I didn't do, once upon a time.) She asked me if I had experience of electronic cash registers, and I told her I did but that I imagined they had advanced considerably since I had last used one. Margaret said she wasn't sure about that, but just having a member of staff who wasn't frightened of the bloody things would be a start. I pictured the old woman with the hearing aid. Margaret asked if I was a recipient of Angel Listening, which I had hoped she would not, and I admitted that I was. She then asked me, in a slightly unexpected tone, if I thought it was doing me any good. I carefully said it was early days and I didn't really know. Margaret then spent ten minutes telling me how she had been short-listed for manager of the Save the Children shop, which was the job she really wanted and had also gone up for Oxfam and Cancer Research but hadn't been successful. She has been running things at the Listening Angels for a couple of years, but she is still looking elsewhere. I heard her light two cigarettes in the course of our conversation. I start on Wednesday.

* * *

Today, for the first time, I e-mailed Rachel, because I finally had some achievements to boast about (Hon. Sec. of the Parents' Committee and getting a voluntary job).

* * *

Kind-faced Caroline approached me at the school gate this morning and, as tactfully and kind-facedly as she could, handed me a copy of my boastful e-mail. Seemingly, I sent it not only to Rachel but also to all of the Parents' Committee. As with when Rachel washed my dirty laundry at her house, the only way to survive this has been to go inwardly completely into denial. However, I do not know how I made the error and must find out, or Rachel and Eleanor will be receiving all the monthly minutes of the Parents' Committee meetings.

* * *

This morning, during Prentiss's visit, he came home unexpectedly because his interview with an interesting character from the small-business community had fallen through. He is privately derisive about the whole Listening Angels thing, so I was relieved that he spoke to Prentiss like she was worth his while, and I ended up suggesting that he interview her in place of his fall-through, and he ended up asking her, and Prentiss ended up saying yes. (I thought she would.) She had to go straight from me to another client, so they have arranged the interview for tomorrow afternoon, and Prentiss is going to kill two birds with one stone by giving him a healing reiki massage, which can count as more of her coursework. I still haven't had a chance to show her my Notes.

* * *

Kind of a special day: my first time working outside the home for a very long while. Margaret couldn't stay, as she had been called away on a training day, so after she let us in and switched off the burglar alarm and switched on the till, I had to find my own way. So far, I have learned that: Lorna is the tall deaf one who keeps guard behind the pay-point, Kathleen is the small white-haired one who does all the steam-ironing behind the scenes, Emily is the big one who isn't actually on the team but spends most of her day getting in their way, and all of them are, as advised, afraid of the cash register.

*

His interview with Prentiss went so well that he was late home. He is very taken with the whole reiki thing and with Prentiss's house, which is a renovation in progress, slightly out in the country, and with Prentiss's *dog*. (He has campaigned strenuously against us ever having one.) Hmm. Prentiss is not exactly my friend, but I still don't feel like having her stolen from me by *him*.

*

An e-mail from Rachel: 'Big wow. Have you reorganised their shop for them yet?' (Actually, I did do a bit of colour-sorting. Quite a bit.) 'Say Hello to everyone for me. And admit you have a problem. Please.'

Of course I admit I have a problem. Admitting it is no longer difficult. *Fixing it* is difficult. Because my addiction seems to be, in a nutshell, *trying harder*, and how can I manage to beat that without, you know, *trying harder*? Get out of that.

* * *

There is a skip outside Pete and Stephanie's house. They are getting rid of all their household rubbish before they move, I suppose. I envy them – their move and their skip. Having a skip outside your house has sort of become a status symbol, hasn't it? It's a sign you're on your way up in the world and you're breaking free of all your old deadbeat stuff and clutter.

*

I felt obliged to work extra hard in our house today, because of swanning about as a volunteer yesterday. (Volunteer working is really a luxury for comfortably off pensioners and moneyed ladies on loan from the coffee-morning circuit, isn't it? And I am certainly neither.)

*

Prentiss Prine isn't allowed to visit me or phone me outside our weekly hour. I wonder if she would, though, were she permitted. (*Why* isn't she allowed to talk to me except for our appointments? I think it's a safeguard in case my emotional neediness overwhelms her.) She's allowed to phone him.

* * *

I spent most of this morning trying to get the printer to print out the minutes of the Parents' Committee meeting so that I can physically hand them round on Monday night, as I have not yet figured out how to e-mail only the committee and not also Rachel and Eleanor. I don't know what I did to end up with thirty-seven documents waiting, and then I couldn't get the printer to stop printing them all in full, even though they were nothing to do with what I wanted. I felt like the Sorcerer's Apprentice, only with pages, pages, pages spitting out all over the floor.

*

Although I have never set foot in Prentiss's home, I'm beginning to feel I know it rather well since his visit there. Apparently, she is living in an old house she has named Ivy Cottage and is doing it up one room at a time. She has great taste. She has painted her kitchen orange and has a wood-burning stove in it and copper pans hanging from a rack overhead, flowers on the table and coffee always perking by the sink. I have had to bite my tongue to avoid pointing out that he has always said that (a) giving houses names is pretentious; (b) old houses are money-pits and, therefore, we are not ever going to live in one; (c) orange is out of the question; (d) oil is the practical home-heating fuel; (e) it's tidier to have everything put away in cupboards; (f) flowers in the house set off his hayfever; and (g) he prefers instant.

*

No Trevor in the paper this week. Is he unwell?

* * *

At the Parents' Committee tonight we spent nearly three hours discussing school uniforms, even though I had typed up and handed round an agenda, which read: (1) Introductions and Apologies (2) Minutes of Last Meeting; (3) Apple Supper; (4) Christmas Fair; (5) Two O'Clock Parking; and (6) Any Other Business. Where was the point in that, then? In about five minutes at the end, the usual people said they'd put out the call for scones and tarts for the Apple Supper, and it was agreed another separate meeting was required to organise the Christmas Fair. The thin father who was almost certainly there to talk about the two o'clock parking barely spoke the whole time but looked frustrated out of his head. He won't be back. In fact, I probably wouldn't bother myself if I hadn't accepted office.

Also! Marilyn is quitting teaching! Instead, she is going to become a market trader. My immediate reaction to this news was that I couldn't imagine anyone less likely to be out there on cold mornings up to her wellies in mud and cauliflowers, but then I realised I was thinking of a market *gardener*. In fact, Marilyn is going to sell funky fair-trade clothing and pencils made out of old vending cups at a stall in the town two days a week. (*I* want to sell funky clothing and vending-cup pencils, but there's no way two people can do it. Why couldn't I have thought of it first?) Marilyn gave the reason for her change of career as boredom. Boredom? Part of me wanted to be self-righteously outraged that a grown woman, responsible for her life choices to date, living in pampered Western civilisation with running water, the National Health Service and low-fat coleslaw, could dare to complain of boredom. Another part of me felt like dancing round town singing it out for all to hear, *I (too) am bored, bored, bored, bored, bored!* In the end, a kind of middle-ground voice won, which reminded me how lucky I am not to be a blind ex-serviceman or a foot-and-mouth painter and advised me to put up and shut up.

When I got home, I tried to do the flyer for the Apple Supper, as I had rashly agreed, and found it went better than expected. My word-processor is like my youngest child. If I say, for example, 'Centre these three asterisks and then leave two blank lines,' the machine centres the three asterisks (so far, so good), then wipes them out and replaces them with a whole row of heavy dashes. This is like when I say to my smallest child, 'Hang up your coat,' and he removes his coat, heads for the peg (so far, so good) then drops it on the floor. But then I say, again, 'No. Don't give me a whole row of heavy dashes. Centre these three asterisks and then leave two blank lines.' This is like 'No. Don't drop it on the floor. Hang it up.' And, wonder of wonders, they are both equally obliging upon the second ask.

This is completely different from my middle child, who will snarl at me and walk away, giving me the fingers, if I ask for anything once, let alone twice.

125

* * *

I was glad to see Prentiss, this morning and, although she still did lots of talking, it was much more probing than before, and she seemed genuinely interested in my replies. Perhaps she has had a training day. She asked a lot of stuff about him and how we had got together and how we got along now – stuff I rarely think about (I try not to). I ended up saying I thought we were both suffering from toxic levels of disappointment, in ourselves and each other. We are neither of us truly bad. We are not actively cruel to each other. It's just years of nothing but trying too hard and falling too short. It wears you down. Prentiss is no longer seeing her on-off boyfriend, Seamus Kelly. She says the relationship is off permanently this time because Seamus Kelly likes being static, whereas Prentiss prefers to grow. She gave him a reiki massage as a leaving gift, though, to show there were no hard feelings on her part. I still don't think Prentiss gets what my problem is. She treats me like a middle-aged woman with depression. Next week, before she takes charge of things, I'm definitely going to show her my Notes for the Next Time. Then she'll understand.

* * *

Lorna was late reporting for cash-register duty today, and Kathleen was almost frantic when a potential paying customer came in off the street. Her fear of having to turn down trade was battling with her doubt as to whether I was *allowed* to work the till, because she, Kathleen, was not *allowed*, she was only allowed to put things into bags while standing *beside* the person who was *allowed*. I asked Kathleen who had forbidden her to operate the cash register, but she played dumb on that one. I suspect Margaret (who was away on another training day – is this why she was so keen for me to work Wednesdays?). With boldness from where I do not know, I declared that, yes, I was allowed to work the till. (At this point, I didn't even know how to open it.) When the customer brought over a shrink-thickened Shetland wool V-neck jumper priced at £1.50, I *grounded* myself, then quietly asked him if he could give me the correct change as the register wasn't working, which he did, and I put it in a saucer on the side. I then took two minutes to read the little instruction cards tied to the till key, sold myself three items as a trial and, lo and behold, I could work the till.

I didn't dare tell Kathleen and Lorna, to whom this charity shop represents the throbbing heart of commerce, that I was once entrusted with thousands of pounds a day of company money to spend on goods at my discretion.

* * *

The reason Trevor wasn't in the paper is that he has had a nervous breakdown. They found him in the store under the shop taking all the shoes out of their boxes. He's in hospital now. I feel like I should go and see him, and I also feel like I shouldn't.

*

Do you know? I think perhaps I *do* greet the unseen with a cheer: I think it's more the 'seen' that gets me down. The one exception is the unseen dog that barks at us from behind the hedge on the days when I walk the children to school. Like most unseen dogs behind hedges, it sounds like a Rottweiler, and I can't see an angry Rottweiler being stopped in his big tracks by me calling out, 'Hello there, fine fellow, and how are you this brave day?'

* * *

Eleanor came round this morning and helped me to do the apple tarts for tomorrow night's annual Apple Supper at the school. Let me rephrase. Eleanor came round and *made* the apple tarts. I was glad, really. They will be the best of any there. Eleanor squeezed lemons onto the creamy apple slices to keep them white and laid them out in beautiful arcs so it was almost a shame to add the lids. She fluted the pastry deftly round the edges, like a picture-book pie crust, glazed the tops shinily with egg and even added pastry cut-outs of apples as a finishing flourish. There are some things my mother does really well.

No irksome smells in our house today. Just the happy, homely fragrance of baking apple.

*

He is doing a lot of evening diary jobs just now. I am watching a lot of two-part crime dramas.

*

The paper seems a little bit empty without Trevor in it, pointing.

* * *

It's surprising how many people want to eat apple tarts in a school assembly hall on a Saturday night. I think it's a hankering after village life. One of these days, all that half-price sofa shopping is going to come crashing down. Eleanor's splendid tarts were used as a sort of centrepiece, as no one could bear to slice them, and we handed out triangles of a much blander appearance from the dinner hatch, along with cups of tea. There was apple-dunking for the children, and Marilyn Softly also had a go. When someone saw that one of her long, blonde hairs had fallen into the water, Marilyn just laughed it off (I would have cringed with embarrassment) and said it was Johnson's baby shampoo, so it shouldn't sting anybody's eyes. Ha. She wouldn't know which shampoo she uses – it's perfectly obvious Marilyn *always* gets her hair washed and dried in a salon. In previous years, there used to be apples on strings, tied from the ceiling, until somebody expressed concerns about gingivitis, so that's gone. Instead, Miss Morning (visiting, looking radiantly well, not everyone spends their retirement fussing over special offers) brought one of those Mexican things the children bash with a stick to get the candy out. No doubt there will be cries of cranial trauma when one of the sweets hits some child on the head.

To be truthful, I'm not great with crowds, but I cope

better when I have a specific job to do, so I was happy enough behind the hatch. He carried the coats, ate his slice of tart and mingled for a while before settling down on a bench in Dads' Corner.

* * *

Out of the blue, just a perfect day. Not like you think a perfect day would be – I didn't win the lottery, I didn't fall in love. It's just that it was Hallowe'en, and the children were off school, so we had a little lie-in, and then with all that skim-tidying that's been going on, the house wasn't so bad to be in, and there was time to make a pumpkin lantern, so we did, and it was a good job, and we set it up in the front window on a little table for all the dog-walkers to see, and for him to see when he came home from work, and we all sat on the sofa with the light fading and the fire burning and the lantern lit, and we watched *Into the West*, and I cried from the very start with the horse in the lift, and this world felt not too busy and as good a place as any in which to live.

* * *

I have shown Prentiss Prine my Notes for the Next Time. I did it at the kitchen table when she'd finished her coffee. I cleared her place, wiped it clean and set down the folder. There was a time when I felt a kind of twisted pride in my strange portfolio, but ever since the day Rachel found it, such feelings have gone for ever. I flicked through some pages for Prentiss: Angel Costumes, Barbecue, Birthday Parties, Bolognese (with no Bits), Christmas Cake, Christmas Cards, Christmas Decorations, Christmas Presents, Christmas Tree, Dalek Costume, Dusting, Egg Custard, Fun Day . . . For once, she was speechless. Anyone would be. How would you react if someone handed you a neatly (*very neatly*) typed, poly-pocketed manual of how to do everything perfectly, based on all the lessons they had learned from all their mistakes so that they and/or posterity need never make those same mistakes again?

It is my only means of making my failure bearable. It redeems every wrong road with the promise of the right one next time.

Prentiss put on her lovely glasses and turned over a few pages for herself – Santa Claus, Tombola, Umbrellas – reading silently a bit here, a bit there. After a moment or two, she said, 'Oh. My. God!' And then: 'May I Xerox this stuff?'

Prentiss, you really aren't getting it.

*   *   *

There isn't an awful lot to do in a minority charity shop down a side street with a staff of three, one of whom is a steam-ironing dynamo. After you've Hoovered the carpet and shone up the glass and hung out Kathleen's garments, you have to find a way of passing the time until there's a customer. So we invented the Off-Licence Game. It isn't complicated. We eye up shoppers going into the off-licence across the road and guess what they're going to buy. The check-out is in clear view of our window, so Lorna, who can see lots better than she can hear, is able to tell us who has won and who has to make the next round of teas. So far, I'm ahead, but Lorna and Kathleen, who are town natives, have invented their own subsidiary game of oohing and aahing at highly unexpected personages making equally unexpected purchases, sometimes at intriguing times of the day.

I asked Kathleen and Lorna what they would buy if they went into the off-licence. It turns out neither has ever been in an off-licence in her life, but Kathleen has drunk Irish Mist and liked it, and Lorna wouldn't say no to a Tia Maria. That got me thinking, and I asked them if they have a staff do for Christmas, and they said not a do exactly but Margaret always closes the shop for half an hour one morning and takes them across the road to Mumbles, the coffee shop beside the off-licence for milky coffees and mince pies.

Oh, I think this year we can do better than that.

*　*　*

Marilyn Softly approached me at the school gate and asked me if it was true that I knew Prentiss Prine. I felt a bit squirmy – you don't want everyone knowing that you have to buy your friendship – but I admitted that it was. Marilyn wants to have a reiki healing massage and wondered if Prentiss was any good. I rashly confided in Marilyn that I had felt something during my massage and had cried afterwards, and Marilyn looked at me oddly, and I knew I'd given too much away. So then, of course, I realised that Marilyn would ask for Prentiss's contact details, which she did, and I couldn't give them because I am not allowed to contact Prentiss, except through the Listening Angels Trust, and this was what I had to tell Marilyn. Now revealed by my own lips as having to rent a friend, I wished to be swallowed by that infamous hole in the ground.

* * *

Terry came round to show off his buy-one-get-one-free varifocals. He kept nudging the children and nodding at me, trying to get them to say the words, 'She should've gone to . . .' you-know-where. Why doesn't he get it? It's not that I don't *know* I'm walking around with more Sellotape than frame on my frames, it's just that I don't have the fucking *money* to go to Specsavers. All right?

*

It was on Zero FM that Trevor has dropped all his cases against his former party and the Sunday papers. It said he had been admitted to hospital suffering from acute stress. I keep imagining the hassle of having to rebox all those shoes.

* * *

I have looked on the Internet. There is nothing about Trying Harders Anonymous.

* * *

The good thing about me is that I always bounce back. I don't know quite how, but it's true. I suppose it's what you could call a 'personal quality'. Some people might say I don't know when to quit, or I'm dead but I won't lie down, and I can see that way of looking at things, but it's rather negative, isn't it? I mean, resilience is a wonderful characteristic. I would say I live in hope, which, in its way, is quite heroic. Unless, of course, it is actually hope to which I am addicted. Oh!

* * *

It is Prentiss's visit today, and I think I owe her some thanks. She may be a bit loopy, but she did me a huge favour in pushing me towards the charity-shop job. Doing my shifts there necessarily subtracts hours available for housework/paperwork at home, so because I have less time I am forced to be less finicky and am probably getting more done. I am almost afraid to think it, but I don't seem to be blinking these days either.

*

Now, here's a thought: what if he and I were to introduce Prentiss to Woods? She could give him a run for his money. And 'massage' is probably Woods's favourite word. We could all become four great friends who get together at one of our houses and sit round drinking red wine and discussing things. (Somehow I have managed to draw an old range cooker and a lot of floor cushions into this scenario, although naturally we have neither.)

*

Boy, is our kitchen ugly! Even gleaming, as it is today, there is no way to make wall-to-wall brown wood-effect Formica look anything other than horrible.

The reason our ugly kitchen gleams today is that Jeffrey Devine was having a phone-in on unusual addictions, which, for obvious reasons, I was very keen to hang around to hear. The range of other people's 'things' was amazing, and you couldn't help comparing which you'd rather have. Would you prefer to be addicted to wine gums, for example, or to fastening the seatbelt on your child's car-seat even when the child isn't in it? Other reported addictions included hand-washing (well known), *bidet*-using (less well known), coffee (boring), sniffing rubber tyres (more interesting) and cutting oneself (tragic). And everyone reported the same thing: the surge of relief, then the slump. Jeffrey Devine's regular counsellor, Dr Susan McPeake, said several therapeutic approaches were available, including hypnotherapy, and that addiction runs in families so anyone with a family member who is an alcoholic, for example, should be very careful how they drink. *Wrong, Dr Susan! Wrong!* You need to listen to Rachel or talk to me. Addiction isn't in the alcohol or the gambling. It's in you. And if you don't give it drink or drugs or money, it will feed on whatever it can find.

* * *

The shop has suddenly become much busier. I have had to take out the second steam iron to help Kathleen keep up.

Margaret says it's always like this just before Christmas – people clearing out their old stuff to make way for the new. Margaret's husband fits kitchens, and he says it's the same in his line: everybody wants to be refitted in time for Christmas, but nobody thinks of phoning him until November. I hadn't thought of Christmas as a time of renewal, but I suppose it is, especially if you stretch it to include New Year.

What will my New Year's resolution be? I wonder. Last year, I resolved to prepare all the packed lunches the night before, which makes it a lot easier to face getting up in the morning. It is the only resolution I have ever kept. He resolved to keep the petrol tank filled to save on evaporation, but I don't think that one lasted beyond January. Wendy came into the shop today with black bags of hers and Billie's old clothing and a chrome juice press that she says she'll never use. I believe her. Wendy's the sort of athletic-demeaned person who looks like she eats fruit with the juice in and the peel still on. Even bananas. She always seems a little bit aggressive towards me – I think because my continuing association with Woods via him makes her feel at a disadvantage. If only she knew: he hasn't been seeing much of Woods lately, and I am pretty sure Woods doesn't even like me. I don't really fit his criteria as a Woman, and I could be perceived as having taken away his friend. *He* was dead against getting Prentiss together with Woods, by the way, so I don't need to feel guilty on that score. Wendy and Billie are going on a skiing holiday *as part of* Billie's Christmas present (!).

We had a new 'lurker' in the shop today. We get them from time to time, in addition to Emily and Shouting Barbara – lonely people with nowhere to go and men who buy used ladies' tights. Today's lurker was a big, youngish, handsomeish man with dark red hair and a red beard. He mainly lurked by the Christmas cards and could have passed himself off as a normal customer if he hadn't stayed so long and sneaked looks at us so much.

Margaret was impressed by the quality of Wendy's cast-offs. So impressed, I noticed, that she left work with a shopping bag although she had arrived with just handbag and keys.

* * *

Philomena was struck by a 4x4 on the no-thirty-m.p.h.-speed-limit stretch of road between Woods's apartment and the school. I meanly wondered why the driver (or vehicle) did not recognise and fear her groundedness and swerve round her. It seems like Philomena has met her match.

*

The postal backlog is making festering noises again, and I have decided on a new approach. I am imagining we had a house fire in which all the old post was destroyed. Would life go on? Well, of course. Does this prove how unimportant the postal backlog really is? I try to say yes and mean it.

* * *

Margaret has telephoned to ask if I can go into the shop on Monday. Apparently, it is going to be Volunteers' Week, and someone from the local paper is coming to do an interview. Margaret doesn't want them to get the idea that the shop is staffed entirely by old ladies with white hair and hearing aids (although, of course, it pretty well is). She thought I would give the right impression and hopefully attract some younger people to the possibility of donating a few hours. For just a moment, I puffed up with a sense of purpose, until Margaret added, in the discreet tone that tells you you're about to be humiliated, that perhaps I would think of wearing 'a nice bright top'. But never mind.

*

I have had an excellent idea. As advertising for the Angels' shop, I am going to wear all items we actually have on sale for the interview on Monday. This will help to undermine the taboo on charity-shop buying, plus it will be a talking point for the interview. It will also overcome the problem of me not having 'a nice bright top' of my own.

* * *

Despite enthusiastic support for my idea from Kathleen and Lorna, Margaret was horrified by the modelling-the-stock plan and only relented when I agreed to stick to the superior garments brought in last week by Wendy. Of course, these were Wendy's old summer cast-offs, so I looked rather unseasonal, but at least the quality was right.

Word of the media attention must have leaked because

we had a phenomenal number of customers from the moment we opened the doors. Margaret was horrified all over again when Shouting Barbara showed up and looked like staying, as well, of course, as ensuring that, if there were still a few shoppers left in town who *didn't* know we were having the paper in, they soon would. Barbara shouted, 'I SEE YOU GOT YOUR HAIR DONE, MARGARET! DID YOU GET IT DONE FOR THE PHOTOGRAPH?!' and Lorna and Kathleen looked at Margaret accusingly because nobody had pointed out to them that there might be a photographer coming, or they might have liked to get their hair done, too.

The red-headed lurker put in an appearance, and I must now consider the possibility that he is a bona-fide customer as he brought us a carrier bag of old duvet covers and pillow cases. (Margaret again looking interested.) However, he does still have a hovering quality, which suggests he wants something but is afraid to ask. I took a basket of tights over and set it beside where he was standing, but that didn't seem to do the trick.

When Janet the newspaper journalist finally arrived, I hung back because Kathleen and Lorna work three days a week to my one and have been there from the start. I busied myself replacing things we'd sold from the window and sorting socks with Emily and let my colleagues have first bite of the cherry. Then Norman, the photographer, appeared, and we all lined up for the photographs – one inside, one out – and then came my turn to be talked to. But Margaret had misled me. I was not of interest because I was younger than the other ladies. I was of interest because, unlike Kathleen and Lorna, I was one of the no-mates misfits who had been sent a Listening Angel. The interviewer wanted to know *what was that like*? Well, what did she *think* it was like? I felt betrayed by Margaret and fantasised throughout the interview of reporting her to the police for stealing Wendy's best cast-offs, then me getting her job and doing it so well that I was asked to be regional manager of all the Angels' shops, then being head hunted by Oxfam. Of course, Janet saw none of this because, on the outside, I was simply a pink-faced, palpitating woman who might just have been nervous or going through the menopause.

Distracted by my burning resentment of Margaret, I allowed myself to agree that, yes, mid-life could be a lonely time for many women who had been home makers; yes, it was sometimes difficult to maintain adult friendships once children came along; yes, it was different for men as they had usually continued to work outside the home; I even agreed that it took a very special kind of person to do the work of a Listening Angel, at which point the interviewer started going on about the skill of 'active listening', and I smiled reluctantly as I thought, Prentiss is more active than most.

After we'd all had our turn, evil spin-doctor Margaret took Janet across to Mumbles to spell the names for Norman's captions and tie up any loose ends.

*

Another meeting of the Parents' Committee, and this time I brought the red book but didn't bother with an agenda. A new husband-and-wife team attempted to talk about the two o'clock parking, but they'd picked the wrong time and definitely the wrong people and were probably amazed when they went home to discover that all they'd managed to do was get saddled with running the Christmas raffle. I suggested we *buy* the hamper this year, instead of asking the parents to contribute one item each (it looks OK on the top with the Elizabeth Shaw mints and the bottle of Shloer, but underneath there are always fourteen tins of red salmon).

Marilyn told me she has been to see Philomena in hospital, and her leg is in traction. How does she ground herself now, then?

Lots of talk. No decisions. I am to send out a note about another meeting.

* * *

Prentiss thinks she is being stalked. By her former lover, Seamus Kelly. She has been getting silent phone calls, and a couple of times she thinks she's seen him outside her house. Seamus Kelly sounds like a nutter. He works in IT and he plays the bodhrán and he thinks he's going to retire to County Clare by the time he's thirty-five. Actually, Prentiss says he probably will be able to retire by the time he's thirty-five because he's making a fortune in IT and he forgets to spend any of it. Prentiss wanted him to spend a bit on fixing her roof, but Seamus Kelly wasn't sure, and now he's dumped. (No connection, Prentiss says.) I made the usual bland suggestions about changing her phone number and going to the police, but Prentiss thinks these will only encourage Seamus to think of her as a victim. Prentiss! A victim! I find that hard to imagine. If you ask me, Seamus Kelly probably forgot his toothbrush and is trying to summon up the courage to ask for it back.

I enquired whether Prentiss is going home to the States for Christmas to see her family. She doesn't know. She said it will be a dry house if her brother is allowed home from rehab, and they have to keep the kitchen locked because of her sister, so Prentiss wouldn't be able to let her hair down. Actually, by 'family' I meant her little son, Ben, but she didn't mention him. Secretly, I think Prentiss has met someone new here. She hasn't exactly said so, but she always wants to talk about falling in love these days, as if it's just falling in love in general, but I don't think it is in general. I think it's in particular.

* * *

Margaret can hardly contain her excitement over our forthcoming exposure in the paper and is going to drive to the printworks tomorrow night and get us a copy hot off the press. She went over to Mumbles and bought butterfly cakes and takeaway milky coffees (on which Kathleen scalded her lip by drinking it too fast through the hole in the lid). I thought the time was right to approach Margaret about a proper Christmas party. She said she didn't know, but she would think about it.

Terry popped in, with two pairs of BOGOF trousers in a bag under his arm, although this didn't stop him taking a look at ours. Of course, he couldn't believe we in the charity shop hadn't caught on to the BOGOF culture and gave Margaret a comedy lecture on the subject, which she loved, and before the day was out she had a sign in the window offering buy one get one free on children's socks. (Admittedly, we do have about 300 pairs.)

Margaret also decided – and I notice she's very good at taking executive decisions that other people then have to carry out – that she was sick of looking at the same old pairs of trousers in the men's clothing display, and she sent me with a bag to Save the Children, Kathleen with a bag to Oxfam and Lorna with a bag to the British Heart Foundation just to get rid of them. Kathleen and I managed to make our drops incognito, but Lorna was rumbled when the woman in the British Heart Foundation recognised her and, according to Lorna, chased her and called her a name!

Wendy was back again, with a load of Billie's old board games she's clearing out to make way for Christmas. In addition to their imminent skiing holiday, Woods has now bought them a trip to Lapland. I would love to take our children to Lapland. I asked how Billie is getting on with her rocking horse, and Wendy laughed and said they might as well have bought her a clothes horse because that's what it's ended up as. I imagined poor Sebastian standing solemnly under layers of inside-out Tammy Girl garments, knowing he was in the wrong place with the wrong people but unable to escape. I want to break in and liberate him. Just in case Wendy's frequent visits to my place of work gave me the wrong impression of her affection for me, she made it clear that the reason she favours the Angels' shop is that we're off the high street so it's easier to park at the door. Good.

* * *

Was I *born* stupid or did I *become* so? (This is my personal version of the nature *v.* nurture debate.) Margaret must indeed have picked up early copies of the paper, because one was stuffed through our door this evening. I am a Page-Three Girl: 'Angel rescued me from hell of loneliness, now I'm giving something back'. I didn't say that! I didn't say anything like it! But there I am, looking like I've said it, plus Wendy will see I'm wearing her old donated clothing. (I forgot to explain to the interviewer about that.) There is a small picture of us all standing outside the shop, blinking into the light, then a horrible blown-up one of me, cut off the end on my own, then a very flattering one of none other than *Prentiss*, to which the newspaper has artfully added wings and a halo! All the quotes from me seem to say that I was miserable and friendless – which I was, but who wants to advertise it? – until the befriending service sent me Prentiss, who inspired me to reintegrate into society. (I'm sorry Kathleen and Lorna, but whatever you are, you are not 'society'.) All the quotes from Prentiss say things like, 'You cannot imagine the warm feeling you get from giving someone their life back.' Prentiss didn't give me my life back! She gave me a great deal of her autobiography and a pretty dodgy healing massage.

* * *

School run excruciating. I really didn't want to get out of the car. Nobody mentioned the article, but you could feel them rereading it in their heads as they muttered hello.

* * *

We took the children to see the Christmas-tree lights being switched on. Another triumph for the council. This year they had 'celebrities' from Zero FM leaping about doing a loud but indecipherable roadshow, with special guests the shivering choir of Riverdale Primary School. The smallest chorister was selected to limp upstage and help the robed mayor to flick the switch, and that would have been quite enough: we didn't need the DJ trying to involve the mayor in a Christmas rap that made even the small child look embarrassed. Every other year, they schedule a visit at this point from a VIP (Father Christmas), but now it had been decided this was old hat, so the switch was flicked, about three-quarters of the lights lit up, and that was that. Quite a few people had been unaware of the departure from the usual Santa Claus format and made a disgusted stampede for the cafés to get warm and complain to one another.

Unsmiling strangers were selling glow-in-the-dark headbands in the traditional festive colours of shocking pink and neon yellow. Some people were saying that up the road in our rival town they were having fake snow.

* * *

As I was doing the flyers for the Parents' Committee Christmas Fair, I idly tapped, 'My house is a big mess' into Google. I wasn't really expecting anything, but wow! It seems I am not an isolated case but part of an international community. All over the world there are women who can't get the housework done and can't figure out why. I was glued to the stories of American 'home technicians' who dreaded their husbands coming in at night to find they hadn't even managed to wash the dishes. Some of them had new babies (ah, well), but lots didn't. Nobody knew where to start. Everybody felt overwhelmed. I loved it. There are websites across the planet – Bangkok, Barcelona, Canada, Dubai. I even had a go at reading a German essay on 'Messie-syndrom' and discovered that '1.8 million humans in Germany have so-called "Messie Syndrome"' – Germans, can you believe it? But the Americans were best. For every kindly sister who comforted her unknown correspondent with 'Housework incorrectly done blesses the home', there was another jack-booted Martha ready to lash into her for trying to dress up her indisputable laziness. Two of them rattled back and forth at each other for days about whether there was such a thing as a

146

'cleaning disability' and, if there was, whether it was funny or tragic.

Of course, sooner or later, there would always be an intervention from someone called Helen, a mother of six with a degree in psychology and a commitment to healthy loving families, proprietor of her own website and personal range of spa and beauty products. I preferred Dee Feated, who got crabby with the housework bullies and ordered the stressed-out non-achievers to 'Sit down every once in a while and take a freakin' load off'. Needless to say, having spent all day reading this stuff, I got nothing done.

* * *

Prentiss knows all about the squalor websites. She says everybody's talking about it in the States. Over there, they call it CHAOS – Can't Have Anyone Over Syndrome (because the house is so messy). So now I have a syndrome. Cool. She asked me if I knew I was getting worse, which was a bit of a jolt because I hadn't noticed, and I kind of thought Prentiss didn't really register the state of the place as she has never passed comment on it (until now). But it turns out I have only been seeing half of the Listening Angel picture. Every time Prentiss leaves my house, she explained today, she has thirty minutes to sit round the corner in her parked car so she can write about me in her notebook. Then, when she's seen all her clients, she has another hour back at the Listening Angels Trust HQ to be debriefed and to update her mentor on our progress. When she explained this, I went off the whole thing a bit. I liked it better when I thought it was just unprofessional Prentiss making it up as she went along.

*

I am going to get a notebook and start writing down things about *her*.

*

Anyhow, I'm not worried about the house because it's coming up to Christmas now, and it always looks fab at Christmas. Over the years, we have collected the best decorations ever and about a million fairy-lights, and we have found that, with the cards up, the fire lit and the big lights switched off to show the little lights, our home looks like something from a picture book. You cannot see the crumbs and stains and do not notice the chipped paint – you just see a kind of magical homely glow. I will say this, we are very good at Christmas. It's not just a binge in our house – we have built up some excellent family traditions, which, if we weren't us, I would at least envy and probably copy.

Meanwhile, I grow in my belief that Prentiss has a new relationship. She says she definitely isn't going back to America for Christmas, and when I suggested that she would, if she could bear it, be very welcome to come and share with us, she looked a little strange. That girl has plans of her own.

And another thing (this was actually the biggest curiosity of the day), when Prentiss was leaving, she spotted Seamus Kelly parked outside our house. She muttered, 'Freak', waved sarcastically at him and got into her car. I get that he's stalking Prentiss, but what I don't understand is why Seamus Kelly is stalking me. The man in the parked car was the red-haired lurker from our shop.

* * *

Poor Kathleen. Her rotten son and his wife have just announced that they are going to Gran Canaria to spend Christmas in a hotel. Kathleen is gutted. She thought they were spending Christmas in their own house as usual, with her, and now she has nowhere else to go. Neither Margaret nor Lorna, who have known Kathleen considerably longer than I have, stepped in to offer their hospitality – Margaret said something about going away herself, and Lorna just looked out of the window, so, for the second time in two days, I heard myself asking someone over to our house for Christmas. (And for the second time in two days I got the distinct feeling that the invitation was being declined.) So I can't be suffering from CHAOS after all, can I? Maybe my house isn't as bad as I make out.

We also had a brush with criminality in the shop today. It started with a phone call from Save the Children to say that they were pretty sure they'd had the shoplifters in, but they hadn't been able to make up their minds in time, and, thus, the suspected offenders had got away. The Chamber of Commerce has a protocol about telephoning your neighbours to spread the word if you're targeted by shoplifters, so after Save the Children phoned us, we had to phone the British Heart Foundation. Unfortunately, the elderly Save the Children cashier had been unable to give much of a description of the thieves, beyond the fact that they were two women, so we then spent the morning suspecting all our customers and scrutinising their movements.

This was all right while things were quiet, but then we hit a busy run and also had a problem with a pregnant mother who got light-headed and needed a chair, and we momentarily lost control of the situation. At least, we *thought* she was a bona-fide light-headed woman. Actually she was a decoy. While she was distracting us with her low blood pressure, her partner in crime was loading up with Christmas stock from our giftware catalogue range. She must have thought we were so easy, but she didn't bank on our secret weapon. Shouting Barbara, partly concealed behind the fitting-room curtain, suddenly yelled: 'MARGARET! MARGARET! THIS LADY'S PUTTING THINGS IN HER BAG WITHOUT PAYING FOR THEM!' If the shoplifting woman had decided to charge for the door, I don't think there would have been much we could do to stop her. But it seemed to dazzle her, being 'outed' in such a vocal way, and she dropped her bag and ran, followed hastily by her perhaps fraudulently pregnant co-conspirator. Everybody gave Barbara a big cheer, and

Margaret said she could choose something from the giftware catalogue range, free of charge. Barbara chose a baby's silver bracelet, which was a little sad as it seems unlikely Barbara will ever have a baby. Margaret and Lorna, who had assisted the 'pregnant' woman, were able to give a detailed description of her to the police.

*

I told my colleagues that our lurking redhead is the former lover of Prentiss Prine, my Listening Angel, and immediately I became the centre of attention. (Is this why people gossip?) Margaret said he must really be in love with her, because he couldn't bear to keep the duvet covers that had witnessed their passion and that was why he'd given them to us. Lorna said he was very good-looking (who knew Lorna noticed such things?) and Kathleen said, quite pragmatically, that he just had to get over it. I still don't know why he's hanging around our shop, or if it's me. Does he think Prentiss confides in me – is he looking for a go-between?

*

Our BOGOF offer on children's socks has gone fantastically well. We have almost sold out.

* * *

Prentiss is right. The house *is* worse. I think I've been in denial. The post and the mess and the smell haven't gone anywhere, it's just that I've been finding other activities to hide in. I wish Rachel had stayed. Under her guidance, I could have had this place cleaned up by now. Instead, it's more impossible than ever. I don't know where to start. I could clean the toilets, but that wouldn't get rid of the smell in the kitchen. I could do the kitchen, but that still leaves festering loos. How do I let things get so bad? How do other people manage? *Is* there such a thing as a 'cleaning disability', or am I just kidding myself? And why oh why oh why does all this make me blink?

(I cannot go back to the websites for advice as I know I will only lose another day to *virtually* doing stuff while *actually* doing nothing.)

Our house is like a big dirty animal, stumbling around out of control, and I haven't even the strength to hold it on its leash.

How can I put up Christmas decorations on *this*?

* * *

Jill called at our front door with two black bags of stuff for the charity shop this morning and asked if it would be OK to leave it with me. (As if a couple more black bags of stuff would inconvenience anyone in *our* place. The biggest danger is that they'll get *lost*.) As much to get out of the house as anything, I took them straight round to the shop, where I couldn't be sure if Kathleen looked pleased or disappointed that the garments were all washed and neatly folded and really didn't need any ironing. Until I told her where they had come from, and then Kathleen dropped the bag in surprise, because Jill's husband '*goes with men*'. It turns out that Kathleen is a homophobe! (Not Lorna, though. Lorna told me she had a friend at school called Mildred Faraday whom she loved far more than she ever loved her late husband, and she cried for a week when Mildred went to Canada to be a nurse.) I could see that Kathleen was dubious about even hanging Jill and Trevor's family's clothing alongside everybody else's, as if '*going with men*' was a virus and the other clothes might catch it. Who could have guessed about this dark little cavern in Kathleen's soul?

Unable to face the stinking housework, I hung around the shop for a while, and I was glad I did because we had an unannounced visit from the regional manager. Mrs Nilsson has a relaxed posture, a good haircut and a smoky grey linen trouser suit that's crumpled in only the right places. She gives the strong impression that she knows exactly what she's doing, and the only thing she doesn't know how to do is panic. I want to be her.

What, by the way, is the difference between gazing and staring? I know I sometimes look at people for longer than they are comfortable with, and they feel that I am staring at them, but to me it feels like I am gazing. What I am doing is looking for clues – clues to how someone makes themselves look as they do, or why they are laughing, or how they manage to be happy and successful, if that's what they look like they are. Also, I just enjoy the view – why aren't we meant to? I gazed/stared at Mrs Nilsson, but luckily she didn't seem to mind.

Mrs Nilsson wasn't afraid to roll up her sleeves and get on with things, either. She was particularly helpful to a young mother who was trying to get into the fitting room with her buggy and baby while her other child kept running off and pulling things off the rails. Mrs Nilsson smiled and empathetically told the young woman that her trick was just to communicate a disgusted look to passers-by and pretend the offending child wasn't hers; then she crouched down on the floor and read the little runaround a *Fireman Sam* book from our stock. Kathleen and Lorna loved that. They think Mrs Nilsson is great.

I thought Mrs Nilsson's home life must be very harmonious. In addition to her own attributes, she has the advantage of a supportive husband, whom I have presumed Swedish and whom we can therefore safely say doesn't smack the children if they refuse to eat their meatballs.

I wish we were like that, but we're not. I still haven't got over that morning at the start of the summer when my fuse had burned down all the way to the dynamite because I was trying, trying, trying to get the children ready to go shopping while simultaneously trying to get control of that morning's mess. Eventually, and after much provocation and finding one child still dawdling at the top of the stairs, I *screamed*, 'WHY DOES IT TAKE YOU A FUCKING HOUR AND A HALF TO CLEAN YOUR TEETH?' And I had just about reached the word 'teeth' when I realised that, because it was summer, all the windows were open. And that's about when Jill and Trevor and Pete and Stephanie's children stopped calling round. So this is how I know that mad screaming like mine really isn't going on in other people's houses.

I'll tell you who *doesn't* like Mrs Nilsson, and that's Margaret. She had a face like thunder when she was dropped in on without warning. We soon found out why. Although Mrs Nilsson spoke in low, discreet tones, it is a small shop, and you can't help overhearing when someone is being told off. Apparently Mrs Nilsson has been sending out lots of directives and questionnaires and promotional materials to all the shops in her region, and Margaret has been putting them, unopened, into a cupboard out the back. So Margaret has a professional postal backlog! (I cannot help it if this makes me feel better.) Mrs Nilsson went through all the old post with Margaret, throwing out everything that was out of date and helping her to make sense of everything current, leaving her with just a very small pile to sort out on her own. I wish Mrs Nilsson offered this as a freelance service.

After she'd had a little prowl round the shop, Mrs Nilsson congratulated Margaret on the new colour-coordinated organisation of stock, presumably in an effort to rebuild the monolith of Margaret's ego, which she had just ripped down. This backfired, however, as Lorna and Kathleen couldn't bear it not to be known that this was actually *my* handiwork, for which revelation I was blessed with one of Mrs Nilsson's golden smiles, but I suspect Margaret will have it in for me later.

* * *

We baked the Christmas cake yesterday, as we do every year. And I burned it a little bit, as I also do every year. (We had to bake it in the big fan oven, as the smaller top oven is now so encrusted with pizza drippings, etc. that it fills the kitchen with black smoke, which sets off the fire alarm.)

* * *

Now that I know I'm being monitored, I have made a special effort to clean up the front room in time for Prentiss's visit. I tried to pretend I was Rachel and waded in with two black bags – one for the bin and the other for everything else, to be sorted out later. I also got rid of all the old newspapers from the little cubby under the TV (revealing, at last, the whereabouts of the DVD handset and manual, so now we'll be able to tape things), set the fire, vacuumed, dusted and cleaned the window with a microfibre miracle cloth. On the one hand, I was really pleased to have achieved one fairly presentable room. On the other, once Prentiss was gone, it would be almost time for the first school run and as yet no other part of the house had been touched, I hadn't managed to get in any shopping, or prepare a meal, or do any laundry, so I'm still clueless as to how people manage to fit all these things in every day.

Prentiss immediately remarked on the difference. She actually said, 'Wow! This room is red! I didn't know that!' and handed me a Christmas card. I believe she must make her cards herself because this was a delicate thing, fashioned in pulpy, sage-coloured paper with a hungry-looking green Santa figure on the front. The handwritten greeting said, 'Happy Mid-Winter Festival', so I now have to consider the possibility that Prentiss is a pagan.

As Prentiss was there to dial 999 and wait with me until the ambulance came if I fell and hit my head, I took the opportunity to get the stepladders out and put up the gold card-display strings. Prentiss was amazed that each one was exactly the right length to reach from drawing-pin to drawing-pin along the picture rails. Oh, Prentiss. These are the same strings we use every year and which I coil up and label. I don't mind that we now have four strings up and only one card. I prefer this to what used to happen: cards piling up every day on the bench with the rest of the postal backlog, and none of them on display.

I asked Prentiss if she would put it in her notebook that I had done a big tidy-up and hung up the card-strings, and she said she would.

The room was so nice that in the evening I put a match to the fire, and he and I sat down with glasses of Harvey's Bristol Cream and wrote our own Christmas cards. As I have put in my Notes for the Next Time, I don't hold with selection packs of cards. It's better to pick one really good image and then stick with it. With selection packs, you *can* make a game out of matching up cards and recipients, but you're always left with half a dozen boring village scenes and cats staring out of a window with their backs to you.

There are names on our list that are just names, but there are other names that make you smile and make you want to write something funny or special, because those are people who, once upon a time, really got you, even though you never see them any more. Let it be said, however, that I was proud that, for the first time in years, I had some new names to add to the list, even if those names were Margaret, Kathleen and Lorna. I asked *him* if he wanted to put his own message on Prentiss's card, because he does sort of know her, too, but he said I should write it from all of us.

* * *

Margaret has agreed to a Christmas party! We have managed to grab four places at one of Mumbles' party evenings priced £12.95 a head for three courses plus tea or coffee. (Bring Your Own Alcohol – Mumbles isn't licensed for anything else.) There are three main-course options. To be on the safe side, Kathleen is having the Roast Stuffed Turkey and Honey-Glazed Baked Ham, as it could be the only Christmas dinner she's going to get. The rest of us are free to choose.

I cannot over emphasise the level of excitement our Christmas outing has created in the shop. And I thought I lived a quiet life.

Seamus 'Stalker' Kelly looked in briefly. He's really too good-looking for a weirdo, especially now that he's shaved off his beard.

* * *

Following a phone call from kind-faced Caroline, I popped down to school to help her put together the raffle hamper for Saturday's Christmas Fair. (They did not heed my advice and buy one.) There were only three tins of red salmon, but there were four Bombay Bad Boy Pot Noodles right up against their sell-by dates and a load of unChristmassy tuna. (Some people!) We did our best to bury the less sexy contributions at the bottom and put the After Eights and mince pies at the top, and then I showed Caroline the big length of red tinsel I had brought, and in the end we trigged it up quite nicely. Caroline asked me if I was OK to do the tombola again, and I said I would, because I'm happiest doing one job I understand. (And if you are ever asked to do a tombola, bear in mind that a good one is in great demand and remember the following (and it's nearly time I had recorded a proper Note for the Next Time on this one): (1) Set out all your prizes first, and *then* number them. Do not let well-intentioned people come along and help you to label the prizes randomly because they will be nowhere to be seen when you have a queue of twenty people sighing and rolling their eyes because you can't find the packet of rubber gloves/Terry's chocolate orange/pan-scourers that go with winning ticket 360. (2) Price your tickets to match a popular coin – you won't have time for faffing about looking for change. (3) You need *two* people to operate – one to hand over tickets, the other to hand over prizes. (4) The sweetest little girls are the biggest cheats. *Trust them at your peril.*)

* * *

Something's been going on that I'm not supposed to know about, but now I do. Margaret phoned me this morning after the children had gone to school to say that Lorna had an outpatient's appointment to get her hearing aid looked at and could I by any chance come in to do the till? (Guess what: Margaret has to go on a training day.) I looked at the crumby carpet out in the hall and the buttery fingerprints on the fridge door and thought about another morning spent alone in the house, and I said that of course I would come in, and Margaret called me a pet.

Between just me and Kathleen, we didn't have much in the way of atmosphere (you don't realise what Lorna contributes until she's not there), but we had a go at playing the Off-Licence Game, which was when I saw what I wasn't supposed to see, which was him going into Mumbles and holding the door open for the person who was with him, wearing jeans and boots and a hippie waistcoat, and with whom he was laughing – Prentiss. He looked round, and I stepped back quickly from the window, for reasons that weren't even yet clear to me.

When Kathleen tried to continue with the Off-Licence Game, I couldn't concentrate at first, and then I thought, So what? So he and Prentiss went for milky coffees in Mumbles, so what? This isn't Woods we're talking about. She probably wanted to know how his interview had come out. And that kept me going until they exited Mumbles hand in hand and went straight into the off-licence, and when Kathleen spotted them, strangers to her, and eagerly said, 'What do you think?' I couldn't make a picture in my head where this came out all right, it was all too much for me, and I replied, 'I don't know. I really don't know.'

Evidence

Whether it was a good idea to cross the road to the off-licence and walk in on their hand-holding, laughing liaison, I don't know. On the plus side, it saved any brooding or scheming. It saved any further lies. To give them credit, they instantly dropped their hands and stopped laughing, and they looked so utterly stricken that, for a second, I thought I would start laughing instead. But nobody said anything. I didn't say, 'How could you?' and they didn't say they were sorry. I went back to the shop for my coat and keys, then realised I couldn't leave Kathleen alone with her till demons so was forced to stay and moved about like a ghost, until Lorna came in at one.

* * *

I didn't need to ask him why – I know why. Because Prentiss smells of jasmine and patchouli, and I smell of biological washing powder and fish fingers. Anybody, given a flat choice between fragrant, positive, dynamic Prentiss and grim little, prim little me would choose her. I think I just forgot that 'anybody' could mean him.

*

I am so shocked that I am unable to keep busy/try harder, which gives me more time to think, and I just go round and round in my head with the same things.

* * *

I cannot believe the nerve of that woman. Prentiss came round today for our Listening Angel appointment. It hadn't even occurred to me that she might. When I answered the door-bell in my dressing gown, her cowboy boots were right there on the step. I think I might actually have gasped. She put her head on one side and gave me a sympathetic smile, like I was a child and my dog had just died. She said something about still being 'there' for me and angled herself to come into the house. I grounded myself with roots of steel and blocked her. 'Prentiss,' I said, 'just go away.' She started talking again, but I shut the door. Prentiss shouted through the letterbox: 'You won't tell the Trust about this, will you? I really need this job.'

*

Oh, the humiliation of having no money. He has left us in mind and spirit, but as Prentiss hasn't agreed to full-time custody of his body, he's storing that with us. We do not have the means to provide him with his own flat. I wish he would go away properly, so that I wouldn't have to listen to the drip, drip of information and confession. Today's titbit was that Prentiss really is part Native South American. She would be. Her Inca name is Pachama, which means Mother Earth, and her little son Ben's is Laughing Boy. His children, ours, have reacted to the changing situation predictably: the eldest one cried hysterically for one night, the other two continued playing their games; now all three want to go to Prentiss's house to visit because he told them she has a dog.

*

I have e-mailed Rachel. My pride did not enjoy doing it. I hate needing her, but I could really use some of her sparky wisdom.

*

Pete and Stephanie have gone. They must have moved out today while I was working at the shop. Stripped of curtains and knick-knacks in the windows, their house suddenly has that vacant look. I didn't get to say goodbye.

Just for tonight, the children can make as much noise as they like.

* * *

Why am I so stupid? Does my capacity to embarrass myself know no bounds? I have e-mailed all eight of the Parents' Committee details of his infidelity and my discovery of it.

The humiliation is unbearable. Just to put the tin hat on things, Rachel's computer sent me nothing more than an automated statement saying she is away from her desk doing her Christmas shopping at the world-famous Christmas markets in Germany and will answer my e-mail personally on her return.

*

If there were a bright side, it would be that nothing that is going on here will be in any way redeemable as Notes for the Next Time, as I have no fucking idea of the perfect or even the vaguely right way to handle it when your charity-funded companion, who is supposed to stand between you and suicide, runs off with your partner.

* * *

Just when I think nothing my parents do can surprise me, they find some other way to prove me wrong. Having received her inadvertent round-robin e-mail with all the rest, Eleanor has reconciled with Terry so that Terry can move back home and lend *him* the beach flatlet. It'll be a bit of a commute for him, and I'll have to start walking the children to school every day, but it will also be a big relief all round.

* * *

I went into the shop today to apologise to Margaret for going AWOL before and to ask if I could work some extra hours. I don't want to spend any more time in the gloom of that house by myself, and all the rushing about trying to make it better seems a waste of time now. She asked me if everything was all right, and my voice started to stick in my throat and my eyes began to leak. It was the first time I had cried since seeing the pair of them outside the off-licence, and I thought I would never stop. Margaret looked a little bit sorry she had asked but was kind nevertheless, and so it all came out. When I explained how I had 'caught' them, Margaret looked worried again, as if I might sue the charity shop for being at fault, but I assured her it was a good thing I had found out and pointed out that I couldn't keep crying for ever.

To demonstrate her sensitivity to my situation, Margaret allowed me to use the pricing gun, and I stayed all morning working quietly beside Kathleen, behind the scenes. Kathleen's husband left her for two months in 1954, and she still doesn't know where he went or what he did. She never asked him, and he never asked her what she spent the money on when he found out she had sold all their premium bonds. She only cried twice during that whole episode – once the night he left and once the night he came back. What was she trying to tell me?

*

My co-workers at the Angels' shop seem to understand that the days of playing the Off-Licence Game are over, and we have had to look about for something else to fill the hours. This morning, we changed the window display to something more Christmassy. We dressed the mannequins all in green and red and laid out the last of our range of tree decorations. I wondered inwardly if Christmas would be ruined for my family this year because of our broken home. I also wondered if it would be totally inappropriate for me to give Prentiss a present, because I may be the one person who knows she really wants an ionising salt lamp for her bedside table (you can forget about him taking a hint), but then I remembered that I hate her, and if anyone deserves a good present this year it is me, not her. The traitorous children are going to meet her on Saturday. I don't blame them for going, I just blame them for being excited.

*

Eleanor popped round with a tube of toothpaste, a packet of Twix fingers and a pepperoni pizza – today's spoils of my father's BOGOF shopping. When I asked how they were getting along, she rolled her eyes and said, 'Mamma mia!'

*

I telephoned Caroline to tell her I cannot face returning to the Parents' Committee meetings after my e-mail nightmare. Initially, she tried to act like there was no need for me to be embarrassed, but she ended up saying she would feel the same herself and that she had struggled to face people for weeks after finding out she wasn't invited to

Miss Morning's do. She asked sheepishly if she could have the red book back to pass on to the next incumbent. I said I'd bring it round. I don't want her seeing/smelling the state of the house. The children still won't let me throw out the Hallowe'en lantern, and the whole place stinks of rotting pumpkin.

*

I am worried about everything regarding Saturday's visit to Prentiss. I am worried that, in an ecstasy of love, he will drive too fast on those winding roads where she lives; I am worried that he won't check the children's seatbelts properly; I am worried Prentiss's dog is a killer; I am worried she will shout at them if they won't eat their food (and they won't); I am worried she will have hard corners on her hearth, and scissors and medication left unattended. I am worried that, by accident or design, this thing with him and Prentiss is going to take my children away.

*

Trevor and Jill were out walking. He looks smaller. Smaller than he used to be, and also smaller than Jill. I wouldn't be human if I didn't wonder whether the allegations about his sexual orientation were true – and where does that leave a marriage? Has Jill lost her husband in mind and spirit, too? She was swinging her arms in a determined, toning sort of way. Trevor trailed along like he'd been forced to be there. If he'd stopped and pointed at himself, it would have had to be captioned, 'No Enthusiasm'. Poor Trevor.

*

Terry has bought himself a clarinet. Eleanor will go spare. Some people just aren't cut out for retirement – it leaves them with far too much time on their hands.

* * *

Marilyn Softly came into the shop today. To see me. At first she seemed apologetic – for having requested the contact details of a person she later learned by e-mail was his illicit lover – but then she said, 'I haven't forgiven you for trying to wreck my party' (I didn't try to wreck anything!) 'but I thought you deserved a little treat, so this is my gift from me to you.' And she told me who Prentiss's family tree actually are.

Of course, the children had a fabulous time at Ivy Cottage on Saturday. Prentiss baked cookies and let them eat them all, and they took her dog, Earl, for a walk in the field beside the house and made him his dinner. She also provided them with sketchbooks in which she managed to get them drawing Earl and the cottage and their father and *her* instead of the endless bloody fighting creatures they draw when they're at home. They didn't find out much about Ben, and seemingly there are no photographs of him because Prentiss doesn't need pictures when she keeps him 'in my heart'. Yeuch. But thank you, Marilyn, for my gift. Prentiss

Prine, née *Breen*. (Prine is Ben's father's name.) At first I
didn't get it. *Breen?* I didn't think I knew any Breens. But
Marilyn did. Good old Marilyn. Barbara Breen. Shouting
Barbara. Prentiss's cousin is Shouting Barbara. And, you
know, Prentiss does sort of shout when she talks, too.

*

I am going to make a little Christmas choirmouse. The
craft shop beside the Angels' place has one in the window.
It is made of grey felt with a little red robe and a little white
broderie-anglaise surplice, and it doesn't look too difficult.
It's been ages since I did anything like that.

*

I seem to have lost one of the little teardrops from my
glasses, and the metal now digs into the side of my nose. I
am worried that one of the children will find the teardrop
and eat it, as a sweet.

*

Mumbles isn't good enough for him any more. He has
gone over to the new *baguetterie* with the stupid name on
the main street. He wanted to have a three-way meeting
there (him, me and Prentiss) to discuss arrangements for
Christmas. He said, 'We could meet up in Sandwich
Sandwich,' the *baguetterie*. I said, 'What – for some Lunch
Lunch?' There's nothing to discuss. The children will be
where they've always been at Christmas – at home with
their tree and their presents.

*

173

The children would love that little felt mouse. I could make them one apiece, each ever so slightly different.

*

Eleanor asked me round to look at the clarinet. She took it out from under the bed, opened the case and said, 'What is that?' I said it was a clarinet. She said, 'Yes, that's what he said it was. But I've heard a clarinet before and it didn't sound like this.'

* * *

Tuesday morning used to be my Angel morning. No Prentiss. (No cry.)

(Will I be reassigned another Angel, now that Prentiss doesn't come? Has she even told the Trust that she has stopped visiting, for that matter, or does she continue claiming her £6.59 plus mileage in respect of me? And if so, what does she write now in her notebook?)

*

Lorna has made it her project to find me a replacement pair of spectacles from among the jumble that comes into the shop, but she has no concept of anything other than reading glasses where only the frames need to fit. Lorna, deal with the log in your own eye – or, in your case, ear – before bothering yourself about the mote in mine.

*

The woman in the craft shop didn't have a pattern for the

little felt choirmouse. She said, 'It's so easy you don't even need one.' So then I got to thinking that a choir of three was still quite meagre and ended up buying enough cloth and stick-on eyes to make a total of six little fellows. I'm going to sew them at night when the children are in bed and then magically produce them at an appropriate moment. That's one good thing about being cuckolded: your evenings are largely your own.

*

The children want to know why they're not invited to Ivy Cottage this weekend. They are ready to start behaving like a reconstituted family, but he and Prentiss aren't quite there yet. Prentiss is going away to a past-life regression workshop on Saturday, and Sunday will be Christmas Eve.

*

I let Lorna fit two pairs of reading glasses on me. What's the point of trying to explain?

*

Tomorrow night is our work Christmas do. Despite the fact that (a) my relationship has just broken up; (b) I have announced this to the world by e-mail; (c) my children are keen to spend time with my successor; (d) my house is an unruly mess, malodorous with rotting vegetable; (e) the 'work' in question is unpaid, unskilled and – frankly – uninteresting; and (f) the do is four seats in the coffee shop across the road from our shop, pretending to be a restaurant for the night, I am looking forward to it and am almost excited.

*

I have observed our new next-door neighbours. They were hanging a holly and ivy wreath on their front door. They are an older couple. She wears glasses and looks a little bit like a plain-clothes nun. He is tall and could almost have been good-looking except that he has a slightly elongated head, like Postman Pat's. They waved to acknowledge me, but barely smiled.

* * *

I have unofficially been appointed the musical director of the charity shop. As we are down a side street, we can only just hear the Christmas tunes emanating from speakers in the main square, so I brought in a CD player and a selection of festive music of my own. Kathleen and Lorna couldn't have been more impressed if I had played all the instruments myself. Kathleen's favourite is the Choir of Trinity College, Cambridge ('Wachet auf', 'The Coventry Carol', etc.), while Lorna dotes on Brownies, Guides and Rangers ('Away in a Manger', 'Ding-dong Merrily on High'). Margaret looks vaguely disapproving, as if she's trying to come up with a reason why we shouldn't be doing this but can't quite think of one.

Stalker Kelly popped in and pretended to look at our newly thinned rail of men's trousers. I felt like putting him

out of his misery and telling him that I now know of
Prentiss's affair, but I couldn't quite figure out a way of
initiating such an exchange, so I settled for smiling
sympathetically/knowingly and hoping he got the message.

And Barbara came in with her baby. At first, the sight of
Shouting Barbara backing into the shop with a pram nearly
caused all four of us to keel over. We were all thinking the
same things: social services! Newspaper headlines! What
were the midwives thinking, letting her out? We didn't even
know she was pregnant! The little silver bangle! Barbara
must have had . . . intimacy with a man! She'll drop it! Or
not feed it! Or give it a cup of tea and scald it! Who should
we tell? Yet we made polite exclamations of joy and peeked
into the pram, where we found a sleeping blonde baby doll,
wearing a little silver bangle.

Barbara told us that her baby was called JESSICA and
she had got her on MONDAY. She bought the PRAM in
the SALVATION ARMY SHOP, where she had also
bought a COT. Barbara had found it tiring wheeling the
pram in and out through her usual shop doorways,
however, and she thought she could come into our place
and SIT DOWN for a little while, which she did. I
wondered how far the charade went. Did Barbara buy baby
food, for example? Did she bath Jessica?

Barbara knew her baby was a doll, she said. And we
knew, as she carefully lifted Jessica from the pram and sat
rocking her in a blanket, that Barbara loved her.

*

Even I knew it would be unacceptable to turn up to a Christmas-party night in tracksuit bottoms, so I borrowed a slightly too-big skirt and top from Eleanor as the less embarrassing alternative to borrowing something from the shop. We met up in the doorway of our own premises – Margaret, Kathleen, Lorna and I – then crossed the road to Mumbles, which was blasting out Christmas-party favourites.

As we were going in, I bumped into Jill, looking beautiful, and it turned out that Trevor's shop was having its Christmas do in Mumbles, too. Shouting over the 'background' music, we quickly ran over the 'civilised' subjects of children's Santa lists, how miserable and unfestive the weather was, who was celebrating Christmas where (I had to gloss over that one a bit) and the ridiculous amount of money it all costs (which I don't believe: I'd spend every last penny on Christmas if I thought it could get me that rocking horse). The small talk exhausted, we went our separate ways, only to despair silently, after looking at the seating plan, that we had used up in two minutes what we should have strung out for the next two hours, as we were placed side by side at the party tables.

Trevor was there, too, looking a little better. Perhaps people had been showing him some festive friendliness, or perhaps he'd simply started on his Bring Your Own. I knew Kathleen and Lorna wouldn't have thought to bring anything, and probably wouldn't have ventured into an off-licence even if they had, so I had bought them their bottles of Irish Mist and Tia Maria as Christmas presents, which I handed over now, for immediate application. There was much oohing and aahing, and I was a little concerned at the seasoned drinkers' measures they poured into Mumbles' stout wine glasses, but they were adults, and they probably would have been all right if it hadn't been for Margaret's managerial generosity in providing wine for all, which, mixed with the liqueurs and the melon fan and the Christmas dinner and the Christmas pudding with brandy butter, resulted in Kathleen vomiting on the pavement at 10 p.m. and Margaret and I having to take her and a green-at-the-gills Lorna home in a mini-cab.

When we had seen the two of them safely to their doors, the choice was whether Margaret or I would be dropped off next. I discovered that my fear of Margaret insinuating her way into my house and witnessing its state of near-dereliction was greater than my fear of being left alone in the mini-cab to be attacked and robbed by the driver, so I insisted we drop her off first. When I got home, I phoned Eleanor to see if the children were all right. She said they had been fine and were all sleeping. (Does she drug them?) So. Not a great night out, and no one had even missed me.

* * *

Something I like about him is that he isn't mean about Christmas. He drove twenty-five miles on poor roads just to get us a really good tree from the forest park instead of lifting one of those dried-out, wizened-up things stacked

179

outside the garage shop. He does this every year and appears not to mind, but I hadn't thought I could bank on any such thing on this occasion. For possibly the first time ever, we erected the tree without a cross word. This is almost more conclusive than finding out about his affair or him taking the children to Prentiss's house. Also, for the first time, the fairy lights lit up right away. And there must be about 500 of them.

I think of people receiving our Christmas cards, with all our names on them. They won't know. There should be a big jagged line separating his name from ours. (That's assuming the children choose to stay with me.) (!!)

He is on holiday from work and offered to come round tomorrow and help me get the house tidied up for Christmas. I can't afford to be proud. I need his help. I said, 'Yes, please.'

* * *

We closed the shop at noon today and went across the road for milky coffees and mince pies. That's us on holidays now. Kathleen gave me a pink nightie, and Lorna gave me a box of assorted shortbread. I was touched. Margaret gave us each a Boots bath gift-set, and we gave her the sewing basket we'd clubbed together and bought from the craft shop. It did not escape me that, despite its being the worst Christmas ever in one way, it was also the first Christmas for a very long time that I had received presents from friends I had made by myself and not just from people to whom I happened to be related.

When I got home, he had already let himself in and made a start on the excavation. I could have thrown a hissy fit and demanded the return of the key, but his intrusion was already proving very productive. The pumpkin lantern was gone, if not yet the smell, and the kitchen surfaces were beginning to be visible. One of the squalor websites says some messy people can only function effectively when they have a 'body double' present, and I think maybe that's what's going on with me, because I had been much better when Rachel worked alongside me, and now I could see that I was much better when he was there, too. We got the whole downstairs cleared up, Hoovered and dusted, and he said he'd come back tomorrow and give me a hand with the upstairs, too.

If only it could have been like this when he lived here. (He might not have been so desperate to get away.)

* * *

Today, I did something I really wasn't expecting to do. I walked Prentiss's dog. Not on my own, of course – with him and the children. He had agreed to take Earl for his walks while Prentiss was away at her workshop, and, after us getting on quite well cleaning the upstairs, he asked me if I'd like to come, too, when he was about to set off with the children. It was too good an opportunity to miss. However much more self-respect it might have demonstrated to decline, I couldn't help thinking how gratified I would feel if I could see and touch and have access to Prentiss's world the way she has had access to mine.

Prentiss's place was as he'd described it – kind of cosy and Bohemian, and trigged up more with flair than with money, which it hurt my heart to admit. Of course part of me wanted to vandalise it, wanted to pull down her wall-hangings and drapes with my bare hands, wanted to start a fire, but another part of me wished I could hire her as an interior designer (and if she'd any sense she could do that for considerably more than £6.59 an hour).

*

Tonight, the children begged him to stay over, and, to please them, we both agreed. I took some satisfaction in sitting up on the sofa until I had cut out and sewn my first mouse, which meant he had to wait politely for three hours before he could unroll his sleeping bag and get to 'bed'. As I worked, we watched an old Christmas episode of *Porridge* on BBC2 and talked about Christmases past, and I told him a little bit about Lorna and Kathleen and Margaret and Mrs Nilsson, and he seemed genuinely intrigued. (I didn't tell him about Seamus 'Stalker' Kelly.) We drank two glasses each of Harvey's Bristol Cream and ate a small packet of pistachio nuts before, eventually, I had to slide the finished mouse surreptitiously into my sewing basket so he couldn't see the result. (A flop-necked, lop-sided mess – *that* was why I hadn't made anything like it for so long.)

* * *

Christmas Eve. The best day of the year, in my opinion. At least, it used to be. There's always a bit of last-minute rush – sticking the marzipan on the slightly burnt cake (a week late), mixing the royal icing, scooting down to the garage shop for an extra bag of logs, dashing out for batteries for the children's you-know-whats. This is the kind of bustle I love. And all to a soundtrack of carols.

We have been quite civilised about the broken-home family arrangements for Christmas. He will stay here again tonight, to be *in situ* when the children come down in the morning to see what Santa has left them. (This time he will bring down the Z-bed to the study so as not to disturb Father Christmas at his festive work in the front room.) He will stay for Christmas dinner, then go to Prentiss's for the rest of the afternoon/evening. This means he will miss the ritual opening of family presents round the tree after our meal, but that is his free choice.

I am not flummoxed by turkey cooking-times etc., at this time on a Christmas Eve. The reason is quite simple: Eleanor and Terry come to us every Christmas, and every year Eleanor brings the bird (I wouldn't know one end of a giblet from the other), *he* prepares the vegetables, and all I have to do is the raspberry trifle. (Which I do very well. If you are ever required to make a raspberry trifle, then I give you this one essential note: don't put any of it anywhere near a fridge. This way, everything is slightly soft and yielding and the flavours are much better than if any part of the trifle has been chilled and rendered tasteless and firm.)

*

Miss Morning has left a message on our answerphone wishing us a merry Christmas and asking me if I would help her to organise Marilyn Softly's leaving do. This is either utterly snide (if so, totally out of character for Miss Morning), or superb peace-making (much more in character, as Miss Morning has the character of a true angel). Miss Morning says the do won't be until after the Christmas holidays, but she just wants to get me thinking of ideas at this stage. I have just one idea: invite *everybody*. This is the only idea you really need. I have to wait until I am feeling brave to return the call. That's just the way it is with me and the phone sometimes.

* * *

After an idyllic start to Christmas morning (frost, children delighted with their Santa presents, the house looking good by fairy light), I had a little episode when it was time for him to go. In a gesture of festive goodwill, I went outside to the front wall to wave him off, and, as the car pulled away, I realised once again that he wasn't mine any more and that there would be more and more exits like this because he had someone else to be with now, while I did not. Suddenly the tears came, trickling down my face behind my glasses. I was afraid that the children or my parents would see if I turned back to the house, so I had to stand my ground, waving, pretending he was still there, even though the car was out of sight. I was trying to stop my shoulders shaking, trying to take deep breaths to halt the tears when I was happened upon by the new next-doories returning from their post-prandial stroll. (Do they not know you can get a thrombosis from a frosty walk after a heavy meal?) It turns out they are called Tom and Lucy, and they are very kind.

Tom and Lucy took me into their front room, and Tom fetched a glass of water while Lucy sat with me. Lucy's speech is a little bit German-sounding, but she explained that this is a quirk that has emerged since she had a brain injury and had to relearn how to talk. Lucy and Tom took early retirement after Lucy's illness and now intend, like Voltaire, to cultivate their garden. However, Lucy worked as a therapist before her brain injury, and she still does a little bit of selective work. She told me if I wanted to talk to her, I would find her an excellent listener. Kindness makes me cry more than almost anything – plus: look what happened the last time I signed up for listening therapy. So now Lucy and Tom must wonder what kind of nutters they've moved in beside.

* * *

Kathleen phoned to say she'd had the best Christmas ever on the men's ward at the hospital. (Kathleen's husband practically lives there, it seems.) The nearest she could get to a traditional Christmas dinner was a cold, hard turkey and cranberry sandwich from the chiller in the hospital shop, while her husband was given the full roast-turkey works, but

Kathleen said the atmosphere was great and the nurses were a dead laugh and that, at the end of the day, she was able to take herself off to the toilet whenever she wanted to while her husband had to stay in bed and pee in a bottle.

*

He took the children over to Prentiss's this afternoon. They had bought a new bowl and dog chocolates for Earl, but it hadn't occurred to them to buy anything for Prentiss. Ha-ha. While they were away, I knocked on Tom and Lucy's door and, as unintrusively as possible, casually asked if Lucy had any particular times that were better than others when I might possibly be able to avail myself of her excellent listening skills. Lucy brought me in and gave me some sort of rum-punch drink in a blue pottery goblet. The strange thing about Lucy is that she does all the kind stuff but without much real smiling. It slightly unnerves me. Then Lucy listened as I explained about the break-up and Prentiss's part in it. I hoped that she would be outraged, as a sort of co-professional, by Prentiss's lack of ethics, but she didn't make any comment. When she eventually did speak (when I let her get a word in edgeways), it was to say this: if I wanted change in my life, then I had to change my behaviour; and if I wanted change in my behaviour, then I had to change my beliefs. So, it's my *beliefs* that are at fault, is it? Somehow, I can't see that *believing* he and Prentiss have decided better of their partnership will make it so. Could Lucy's brain injury have affected more than merely her speech? I go back for my next session in a week.

* * *

Marilyn Softly phoned me to say she is doing some market research for her forthcoming ethical market stall, and would I take a look at some products? I said I'd be glad to. She asked if I would prefer to go to her or her come to me, and I asked her to come to me, because this is the one week in the year when the fairy lights and the cards and the decorations and the fresh mess of new toys makes our house look pretty good. She's coming over tomorrow.

* * *

Marilyn brought round her samples. I made a pot of cafetière coffee and tried to look as if we drink cafetière coffee all the time, when, of course, we actually drink instant. Unfortunately, I betrayed my unfamiliarity with the gadget by putting the lid on the wrong way round and then being unable to pour anything out because the spout hole was turned round to the back.

Marilyn's samples were great, and she was very interested in my suggestion that she carry a line in wind-up radios. Her stall is going to do really well. More than ever, I wish I had thought of it first.

* * *

Marilyn is not the only woman to have launched herself into business. When I took one of the children into town today to replace his black school shoes for the start of term, I found that Trevor's shop has now become Jill's. That is to say, in Trevor's absence, Jill has taken over the running of the place, and she's gone through it like a dose of salts. She still has the leather brogues and zip-up slippers, but they're keeping a low profile at the back of the shop. Meanwhile, she has filled the window with piles of good-looking ladies' designer footwear, and she told me she is opening a brand new teens department next month. While I was there, a leather sofa arrived, wrapped in plastic. It is for the trying-on area, which Jill has also revamped. Trevor ran the shop based on what had worked in the past (i.e., the 1950s), but Jill is basing her management on the MBA she is taking with the Open University. It seemed impolite to ask how poor Trevor was, amid all this progress, so I didn't. But I hope he's OK.

*　*　*

New Year's Day. I used to like New Year's Day. It was like the slate was being wiped clean. Last year's mess would no longer be held against you. You were free to try, to hope again. But that's not much use if I'm addicted to Trying Again or Hoping, is it? It would be like an International Beer Day to an alcoholic. I'd be better off staying in bed with my head under the duvet. Which is pretty much what I feel like doing anyway.

Perhaps I will talk to Lucy about this tomorrow. I've already told her about the whole break-up thing and feel obliged not to bore her with it again, so I must come up with something new.

Eleanor says it's early days, but she thinks Terry may have broken his BOGOF compulsion: he hasn't had a single shopping episode despite the January sales. Unfortunately, his path to salvation has been the discovery of his clarinet, which he now plays constantly and which Eleanor reckons will send her round the bend even faster than trying to find houseroom for all the double purchases. I suggested she buy a shed. For the first time since . . . possibly *ever*, I made my mother's eyes light up.

* * *

Lucy has started to see me in the study at the back of their house. She was on about something to do with 'evidence'. I couldn't concentrate very well because of the bale of paper under her computer desk being upside down. I could barely take my eyes off it, turning the upside-down writing the right way up over and over in my head. I even wondered if Lucy had placed it that way as a test. It took all my will power not to rise from my seat and correct it. Walking out of that room and leaving behind the upside-down packet of paper was very, very difficult. It was the tins cupboard all over again.

* * *

Back to work and to an announcement that Mrs Nilsson will be coming in tomorrow to talk to us about something so we

189

all need to be there. Margaret acted like she knew what the something was but wasn't at liberty to tell us, but I don't believe she actually has a clue. On her coffee break I noticed she was reading the job ads at the back of last week's paper.

Lorna had had what sounded like a quite boring Christmas with her sister and brother-in-law at their bungalow in the country, where the only excitement was her brother-in-law's dark fantasies that every creak and bump about the place was the arrival of intruders to tie them up, beat them with crowbars and steal their building-society books.

Margaret and her (second, it turns out) husband had stayed up till all hours on Christmas Eve/Christmas morning to receive telephone calls from their sons in New Zealand (hers) and Australia (his) and slept away most of the day before going out with another couple for their Christmas meal in a hotel in the evening.

* * *

Mrs Nilsson came to talk to us this morning in a different but equally elegant linen trouser suit. She gathered us round the till area, and I think we thought for a moment that she had come to tell us we were going to be closed down. But no. In fact, the Listening Angels Trust is considering opening drop-in centres attached to some of its shops, and Mrs Nilsson wanted to know whether we thought a drop-in centre could be successfully attached to ours.

Margaret, who I now suspect feels threatened by any

change, immediately jumped in and said we simply didn't have the room. But Mrs Nilsson wasn't fazed. She was a step ahead. Seemingly, there just aren't enough people making little felt mice these days, and the craft shop beside us is going to close. The lease will then be available, and the Angels Trust is looking for indications that a drop-in centre in our town is likely to be viable. I said we had already taken the first steps, being dropped in on pretty constantly by Shouting Barbara, Emily and Stalker Kelly, so this indication at least augured well. Mrs Nilsson said she wouldn't expect Margaret to manage both concerns, which was a tactful shot across Margaret's bows, in case she'd started giving herself any ideas, but she did say to Kathleen and Lorna and me (when Margaret had gone off to make a show of opening her post) that there would be room for movement between the shop and the new drop-in centre, if we thought we might find the variety interesting. At one point, I noticed that she looked long and hard at me – not gazing or staring, more watching – and asked whether the Trust paid me or if I was a volunteer. I saw Kathleen and Lorna exchange a quick what's-so-special-about-her? glance, but that didn't stop me feeling a little bit chuffed that I could pass for the hired help instead of the Angel rehabilitation candidate.

* * *

Of course, all the talk in the shop today is about the drop-in centre. Margaret doesn't think it will work. She reckons people like Shouting Barbara and tramps will drop in first thing and sit around all day drinking the free coffee and putting other people off dropping in at all. Kathleen and Lorna, who had initially appeared excited, seemed to cool at this prospect and said they were happy just to stay working in the shop. So, I pointed out to them that our little town doesn't have any obvious tramps, and Barbara likes to stay on the move anyhow, and they could be like Angel hostesses pouring cups of tea and coffee for lonely people and offering them an oasis of warmth and friendliness in a sometimes chilly world. This seemed to please them, but Margaret looked angrily thwarted. I feel ever more the McMurphy to her Nurse Ratched.

By the time we had finished work this afternoon, Kathleen, Lorna and I had mentally knocked down a bit of wall between the charity shop and the craft shop and created a walk-through archway, designed a self-service coffee bar and devised the soft seating area. (We were all agreed: you cannot unburden yourself on a hard chair.)

*

I suspect three things about Seamus Kelly. (1) He knows that I know about the affair with Prentiss, for he has stopped lurking oddly. (2) He has taken a shine to our charity shop, for he now functions like a normal supporter, bringing us sensible cast-offs in carrier-bags. (3) He is very organised, for he has swiftly brought us all his unwanted Christmas presents (nylon-mix socks in wrapper; popular aftershave, unopened; unpopular paperback, unread).

* * *

A letter came for him today in a long brown envelope with the hospital stamp. It's got to be about his vasectomy. I wonder what's going to happen there. Just because we felt our family was complete (translate as: we hadn't had an unbroken night's sleep for twelve years) doesn't mean that he and Prentiss won't have other ideas. But Prentiss would have to look after this baby. She couldn't go swanning back to the USA and think that *he* could look after it on his own. Our three won't even let him wash their hair.

∗

I have had a hideous thought. If he and Prentiss *were* to have a baby, and Prentiss *did* do a runner back to the States, then who, in light of his incompetence with small offspring, would end up looking after the new half-sibling? No-o-o-o-o-o-o-o! I have only just got my sad ass out of our door and down to the Angels' place for a modicum of adult interaction – I could not bear to be trapped in my chipped-paint box again so cruelly and so soon.

Having previously thought I'd be better off without any resolutions this New Year, I have now changed my mind. At all costs, I resolve to ensure that he and Prentiss do not start a family.

∗ ∗ ∗

I know Lucy assigned me homework for this week, but I can't remember what it is, and my next session is tomorrow.

∗ ∗ ∗

I'm not sure if things are going to work out with me and Lucy. Apparently my assignment from last week was to look for the evidence – 'thu effidence' – that other people's homes are as spick and span as I think they are. Having no friends (apart from the Angel volunteers, and I haven't been in their houses), I could provide no such *effidence*, and Lucy simply would not accept that I *just know*, or that I know from sofa ads and makeover programmes. She looked like she thought she had made a point, but I don't know what it was. Later, at home, I suddenly remembered the sparkling kitchen at Rachel's and wished I had thought of that during the session.

*

When he came round to pick up his post, I tackled him about the vasectomy issue. Apparently I needn't have worried. He is still as keen on this path as ever. Seemingly, Prentiss wouldn't dream of having a child anywhere there isn't provision of Montessori schooling, and there certainly isn't provision anywhere round here. Laughing Boy Ben is in a Montessori school in the States and Prentiss reckons it's the best. I thought, Isn't there another M word, far more important than Montessori, which Prentiss is conveniently overlooking? But I didn't say anything.

* * *

Miss Morning called into the shop to see if I could spare a few minutes for a little chat about Marilyn's leaving do. (She also brought three big bags of immaculate petite cast-offs, which kept Margaret off our backs.) Eddie Softly has said he will pay for hire of a disco, so Miss Morning reckons we just need to find somewhere with a dance floor and a bar/BYO facility. (While she happened to be there, I double-checked with Miss Morning, who would know about these things, that there definitely isn't a Montessori school anywhere nearby. She assured me that there isn't. Phew.)

Lorna and Kathleen remarked on the superior quality of items being brought into the shop since I arrived. They actually said, by 'your friends', so I felt obliged to point out that they aren't friends, exactly, but a neighbour from my street (Jill), an estranged wife of one of *his* friends (Wendy), a special-needs teacher from school (Marilyn) and our children's ex-principal (Miss Morning). Dear Lorna and Kathleen – you don't even realise that *you* are my friends.

* * *

Miss Morning has managed to get Mumbles (!) for Marilyn's leaving party, for nothing. It turns out the young Mumbleses went to our school, and Marilyn was their special-needs teacher, so the proprietors were happy to be involved. Eddie has organised the disco, which just leaves the invitations. As it is to be a surprise party, Eddie is going to pick up Marilyn early from school on Friday, and I have been charged with getting an invitation home with every family. I've explained to Miss Morning that I don't know how to put any artwork or anything on the invitations, and Miss Morning said (knowingly) that she didn't think the

195

artwork was the important thing, and did I? Of course, of course, I did not.

*

The Listening Angels Trust has written to me acknowledging that my service has been terminated and offering me a review to ascertain whether I am still in need of the weekly visits. Of course, my service was only terminated for extraordinary reasons, and not because I had recovered, but when I thought about it, I have Kathleen and Lorna now, and Margaret, and slightly Marilyn and also Lucy. Someone else out there must need a Listening Angel a lot more than I do. So I telephoned the number on the letter and told them to take me off their list. The kind-voiced receptionist thanked me for my call and urged me to ring immediately if I found I was having any problems in the future. I had the peculiar feeling that I had risen one step off the bottom of a ladder.

What am I going to wear to Marilyn's party? Please not Eleanor's slightly too-big skirt and top again.

* * *

Head-splitting difficulties with the mind-of-its-own printer, but ultimately I managed to get a neon-green invitation letter home with every child. (I'm taking no chances on these going unnoticed at the bottom of a schoolbag.)

*

Our children think I'm really important, now, because I was handing out letters in school.

*

Crap. If it's supposed to be a surprise party, shouldn't I have put the invitation letters in envelopes to prevent the pupils reading them and spilling the beans to Marilyn? I can only hope that the 'special' children with whom she works are too 'special' to be able to do so.

*

Jill is in the paper, pointing to her new shop-within-a-shop, which she has imaginatively called Jill's.

* * *

I no longer waken up thinking about him and Prentiss. Now I waken up thinking about what on earth I'm going to wear to Marilyn's do and rehearsing what I can lay before Lucy by way of effidence.

* * *

You don't get to win for long with Lucy. She managed to make me admit that Rachel's house was smaller than ours, more modern than ours, more recently decorated than ours, and that Rachel was a ruthless thrower-outer and was also willing to lie to her children about, for example, the activity of biscuit-eating in order to serve the cause of tidiness in her home. Apparently, it also counts as effidence that Rachel was neither in work at the time of my observations, nor investing in a live-in relationship.

Not because I wanted to pick a fight with Lucy but rather because I still think there are some things you just *know*, I didn't give up. I proposed as evidence all the shelves of tea-light holders and glass pebbles in the supermarket, on the basis that no one accessorises a midden. And, aha, now Lucy was listening. She straightened herself in her chair and conceded (or appeared to) that this was indeed the kind of effidence she was looking for, but *whom* did I see browsing the votives and glass pebbles? Was it the parents with three little boys wildly orbiting their trolleys? No, it was not. It was the smart young couples whose homes were still temples to the fulfilment of their wedding-present lists. (The harassed parents were also present in the supermarket but in a different area, buying *vashing-machine powder und fish-finkers*.)

I get the feeling that Lucy is going to be right a lot of the time and I'm just going to have to get used to it.

* * *

I'll tell you something: these Angels don't fear to tread. When I went into work today, not only was the craft shop gone but the shop-fitters were on site installing a stainless-steel kitchen. Mrs Nilsson was there wearing a blue hard hat that matched her trouser suit. She had called a meeting, I discovered, not only of all the shop staff but also of the Listening Angels for our area. She said she wanted to get an informal idea of how many of us were interested in working at the drop-in centre.

It was the first time I had seen Prentiss since that morning on the doorstep, and there she was, as large as life, still in her boots and all. She stepped forward boldly and announced, 'Prentiss Prine, Listening Angel. Would the drop-in centre work be paid or voluntary?' Mrs Nilsson said that at this stage she was reckoning on a mixture of both. Before I knew it, my hand had slid up, indicating that I had something I wanted to say, too. Mrs Nilsson invited me to speak, and I said – very cautiously, very quietly, but nevertheless I said – 'I don't think it's a very good idea, mixing paid and unpaid staff. I think it might make for resentments.' I dared not look at Margaret, although I could feel her eyes burning into me. Mrs Nilsson said, 'Really?' and, with my heart thumping, I said, 'Yes,' and Mrs Nilsson thanked me for giving her food for thought.

* * *

Lorna and I went to Mumbles after work. Kathleen had to go to the hospital to bring her husband clean pyjamas and a new pack of Steradent.

(In response to the arrival on the local catering scene of Sandwich Sandwich, Mumbles have tried to go more modern and have given all their puddings new cocktail-type names. So now we had to ask for Deep Down and Dirty Mudflat Pie just to get our usual slices of chocolate cheesecake. Good grief.)

Lorna doesn't know if she wants to work at the drop-in centre. It seems to depend on her sister. Lorna is in her seventies, and she still thinks she has to do what her sister tells her. (Lorna wanted to go to Canada with Mildred Faraday and be a nurse, but her sister, who was already married, said someone had to stay at home to look after their widowed mother.) Lorna's sister doesn't think it's nice for Lorna to handle other people's old clothing, but she thinks it's not too bad her being a shop volunteer providing she sticks to the till. Lorna dreads to think what her sister will have to say about her fraternising with down-and-outs, although Lorna herself sounded quite interested in the prospect. I tried to explain to Lorna that the drop-in centre wasn't to be a hobos' refuge but a safe place where anxious or lonely people of all backgrounds could come and be treated kindly and without the usual social expectations. (I *wanted* to tell Lorna that she should tell her sister to fuck off and mind her own business, but families don't work like that, do they?)

* * *

Barbara brought little 'Jessica' into the shop again today. Let me tell you, a plastic baby is a real conversation-stopper. I mean, we can't exactly say, 'She's grown.'

* * *

Lucy's effidence has started to do battle with my pseudo-evidence. Does this mean the therapy is starting to work? Over the weekend, I found that the little inner voices telling

200

me our house is rubbish were being answered back by new little inner voices saying that the parents of three young children are bound to be busy people and asking if it's likely that they have time to do all the wiping, brushing, scouring, Hoovering, dusting, steam-cleaning, defrosting, polishing, washing and ironing that my first little voices seem to think are the norm. However, I am still disgusted with myself for letting three nights' worth of our youngest child's sodden dry pants linger at various locations in the upstairs, so my new top priority in my revamped, newly realistic housework list is putting all rubbish out daily.

*

He has started phoning the children every night, so now he's talking to them more than he did when he lived here. I think when he and I were together, our hearts had become like hard, dried-up prunes. Now he is with Prentiss, his is pink and fleshy and vibrant again, so it is fitter to exercise the love he has to give. I should be glad.

* * *

Ugh. Apparently, I'm still not getting it right. Lucy says I have to stop making lists of things I have to do. She says the really important things are so obvious that I will do them anyway. In my head, I agree, yet I know that without a list to tell me to remove them to the outside bin, I still allowed three nights' saturated dry pants to hang about. What is the matter with me?

Then I thought I would faint with embarrassment when Lucy said she wanted to talk to me about my glasses. I felt to-the-power-of-ten as I had felt when Margaret asked me to wear a nice bright top, and my hand went involuntarily to the gouge on the side of my nose. Lucy practically ordered me to get the money somehow to replace them. 'Ask your mudder and fadder. There is no shame.' There *is* shame! Asking your mudder and fadder to bail you out financially when you're nearly forty? *Of course* there's shame. Isn't there?

Without meaning to, I said that last bit out loud, and Lucy went, 'Hmmm.'

And I said, 'What's "Hmmm"?" and Lucy appeared to think for a time and then asked me, 'Are both your mudder and fadder still alive?' and I said they were, and Lucy seemed to consider this for another while, and then she said, 'Tell me about a time when your mudder or fadder did something wrong,' and I said, 'What – you mean like stealing?' and Lucy said, 'Not necessarily a criminal actiffity. Tell me about a time when your mudder or fadder made a mistake and acknowledged it,' and I thought about this for a while before conceding that I couldn't, and Lucy went 'Hmmm' again, and I said, 'Come on, Lucy, the suspense is killing me,' and Lucy said, *'Let's get zem in here,'* and I thought, Terry and Eleanor in family therapy? I don't think so! And I said, 'They won't come.'

But Lucy said, 'They'll come.'

* * *

Kathleen, Lorna and I have become quite friendly with the builders doing the drop-in centre refit. We make them coffees in our kitchenette, and they share their packets of chocolate digestives with us. They have particularly taken to Kathleen, who stirs in the very sugar for them, and, although it started off as a joke, she has even secretly done one builder's ironing! (I think Kathleen rather enjoyed the subterfuge necessary to keep this transaction from Margaret.) Margaret herself has not entered into these relations and seems less than pleased and rather prickly. I think she preferred it when her staff were predictably lonely misfits and she could be the beacon of functionality; I'm not sure she's so keen on seeing us laughing, eating workmen's biscuits and being happy.

The builders are putting up plasterboard walls to create a large and a small interview room. The small one is for one-to-one counselling, and the large one is for groups. I imagine the interview rooms like something out of *The Bill*, with a desk in the middle and a single stark light overhead, but I don't expect they're going to be like that at all. It would hardly be conducive. Probably it will be carpet tiles and potted plants.

*

Why does it matter that I don't remember Terry and Eleanor making mistakes?

* * *

Miss Morning popped in again, this time to tell me that the invitation to Marilyn's do has been very successful, and she's already had more than fifty RSVPs. I am glad that the event is proving so inclusive but dread the thought of entering such a big crowd alone. I wish I could bring Lorna and Kathleen with me.

* * *

Mrs Nilsson was back, looking as elegant as ever. By complimenting Margaret on the great job she had done in bringing all the post up to date, she managed to make it seem that she was expressing her faith in Margaret by taking the three of us – Lorna, Kathleen and me – out of the shop for the morning and leaving Margaret to run things on her own. (Clever Mrs Nilsson.) She first took us over to Mumbles, where she bought us milky coffees and we told her about the silly pudding names and she laughed at them too (but didn't suggest buying us any, I noticed), and then she said she wanted to get our input on the decor for the drop-in centre. Didn't we feel important! Kathleen favoured a coffee and cream colour scheme Lorna said she liked a sort of heathery purple, and I said I wasn't sure, but perhaps something with a bit more zing if our droppers-in were starting off feeling a bit miserable. Mrs Nilsson listened to all three of us and thought we each had a point and said she agreed that use of colour could be important, and we definitely shouldn't use white because it was rather clinical, which nobody doubted.

Then we went over to the premises to have a look at where the light came in, and the builder whose clothes Kathleen had ironed suggested apple green, and everybody thought it was a good suggestion, especially Mrs Nilsson, who said green was one of the colours available to us for the upholstery of the soft seating, and so it was decided. Then Lorna asked a very pertinent question about toilets, and Mrs Nilsson said it was planned to have one for ladies and one for gents, and Lorna said she didn't think that was enough, because when you're upset – as our clients might well be – you need to use the toilet more, and when you're feeling vulnerable, you just can't wait, and, thanks to Lorna's intervention, there are now going to be three cubicles in the Ladies and two cubicles plus a urinal in the Gents and I don't think Lorna could have felt any nobler at having fulfilled a public service if the council had erected a statue to her in the town square.

(I was comforted that, throughout this conversation, the elegant Mrs Nilsson happily used the word 'toilet', never once suggesting the 'lavatory' alternative.)

* * *

I have no idea what to expect from tomorrow.

* * *

When Lucy announced to my mother, my father and me that she knew what my problem was, I was all ears. When she said my problem was that I was a perfectionist, I laughed out loud although, to be fair, I did think she meant it as a joke. But that's because I thought perfectionists were those people with flawless appearances whose lawns were always mown, windows were always streak-free and cars were washed every Friday. Lucy says this is definitely *not* the case. According to Lucy, perfectionists are the people with ten perfectly labelled biscuit tins because that's something it's possible to do perfectly, but they have wild, messy lives generally because the impossibility of perfection in all things causes them to procrastinate endlessly or just give up.

I experienced such a crisis of recognition I nearly inhaled my tongue.

Lucy said to my parents, 'What would you say iff I said she is dis way because she thinks you neffer made a mistake?' at which point Terry put his head in his hands and wept, and Eleanor looked at the wall.

I keep thinking of Lucy as Frau Lucy, because of her injury-induced weird German accent.

So. It is not exactly with Busyness, Trying Harder or even with Hope but actually with Perfection that I have my abusive relationship.

Ich bin ein perfectionist.

* * *

It turns out Terry and Eleanor made loads of mistakes, which we children never knew about, or else we never knew they were mistakes. For example, Terry made the mistake of not getting the correct help with his obligatory family drink problem in his twenties and, instead spent the next forty years bouncing from one alcohol substitute to another, while Eleanor, rather than admit that her husband was an alcoholic, made the mistake of encouraging this. (She's still paying now – witness the clarinet.) Eleanor's saddest mistake, and the only one to make her cry in the present, was thinking that people regarded her as a trail-blazing working mother until the day she discovered that the other school mothers called us 'the little orphans', which shot her entire career-woman ego down in flames. That was the week she stayed in bed with flu, but thirty years later I learned it hadn't been flu at all.

But what's happened now is the lid is off the bottle, and it's all flowing out. The phone is going every ten minutes with Eleanor or Terry or both admitting to new, undeclared errors: 'I bought you the rabbits even though you were too young to look after them, and then shouted at you when they died' (Terry); 'I made you go swimming in the sea in only your pants because I had forgotten to bring your swimsuit, and you were right, the boys did make fun of you, and I wouldn't admit it' (Eleanor); 'I bought a second-hand Fiat in 1976 even though everyone told me it wasn't worth the money, and in six months it was a bucket of rust' (Terry) . . . and on and on.

I asked them about the glasses. They said they were glad I had brought it up, because there was nothing they wanted more than to buy me a new pair of glasses, but they hadn't wanted to embarrass me by suggesting it. How much more embarrassing did they think this could possibly have been for me than going about with a face full of Sellotape and a suppurating wound on the side of my nose?

(The price was as nothing to them. Perhaps I should encourage my parents to come clean about anything else they think I might be embarrassed by them giving me.)

* * *

Two strange things happened at Marilyn's leaving do. (1) Marilyn asked me to work alongside her on her two-days-a-week ethical market stall; and (2) Seamus Kelly was there! Regarding '(1) Marilyn asked me to help her on her two-days-a-week market stall', I have to say it was a quite drunk Marilyn who sat down beside me, slapped my thigh, asked me if I was enjoying myself (I wasn't), then popped the question. As if to reassure me that normal service regarding previous hostilities would not be affected, she said, 'Don't worry, you weren't my first choice, but Jane Morning turned me down, and I have to have someone to double up for me when I need to go to the toilet.' I told her I'd give it some thought. Does Marilyn know that, aeons ago, I used to be quite something of a high-flyer in the retail world? It wasn't round here. We don't have high-flyers of any kind round here, where, let's face it, the skies are rather too low. So, perhaps Marilyn doesn't know. I think, if I'm to take her up on her offer, it would be best to keep it that way.

Regarding '(2) Seamus Kelly', apparently he did some big IT job recently for Eddie, who runs his own business from home, so the Softlys got to know him pretty well, but this didn't explain why he was sitting at my table. Wearily, I reconciled myself to the realisation that I wasn't going to get out of Marilyn's do without having at least one conversation about the Prentiss Prine scenario, so I took the bull by the horns and spoke to him.

It turns out Seamus Kelly is a really nice man. He was very complimentary about the charity shop, and he likes Lorna and Kathleen, but even he had picked up the vibes around Margaret. He said he thought I had coped really well with what had happened (Prentiss and *him* hooking up), and I asked him what was his *effidence* for that statement, which puzzled him, and I realised I had been rude, talking in my own code, which he couldn't possibly understand, so I quickly said, 'You mean I don't go round stalking people and hanging out in charity shops,' which didn't sound any better, so to remove the need for words, I got Seamus Kelly up for a dance.

Seamus Kelly is not a good dancer, but he's not a bad one either, and the fact that he is so handsome probably makes him look a better mover than he really is, so it's just as well that by that time I had had one and a half glasses of the wine I'd brought or I might have started to feel inadequate. As it was, Seamus Kelly and I had quite a few dances with each other, and then a couple more including a well-gone Marilyn, and when Miss Morning came over and asked if I was all right for getting home, Seamus said he had a taxi booked for midnight and could take me in that. Miss Morning gave me a conspiratorial you've-landed-on-your-feet look, which I pretended not to get because it was obvious to me that Seamus was only hanging round me because of our shared experience, but I told him I was glad of the lift, which I was.

Is it possible that even before I got out of the taxi I heard the phone ringing in our kitchen? And when your phone is ringing at a quarter past midnight, you know you'd better answer it. Of course, my first thought was of the children, and I had desperately fantasised several appalling situations in just the time it took me to charge up the hall. But the children were all right. It was Woods who wasn't. My ex-partner was calling me to say that Woods had been run down on the no thirty-m.p.h.-speed-limit road outside his apartment, and he definitely wasn't all right.

* * *

Only when Woods lay in a hospital bed did I finally figure out that his charm was a virtue, and a currency, and you could take it anywhere, and if you were really good at it, it fed the poor and healed the sick and made people feel fantastic about themselves. And Woods had been really good at it, but I hadn't appreciated it. I had just thought it was worthless smarm. But I was wrong.

* * *

Major cause for excitement in the shop today when a *television crew* came round to film us for the *Sunday Appeal*. Mrs Nilsson was there at nine thirty to let them in and tell us all about it. She said she hadn't warned us beforehand in case it made anybody anxious, but I suspect it was also because she didn't want us dressing up like we were headed for the Royal Enclosure at Ascot, which is what everybody on the *Sunday Appeal* usually looks like, even though they are supposedly training guide dogs or showing young offenders how to plant potatoes. (All the same, it might have been nice for some of us if we could have washed our hair.)

Good though Mrs Nilsson is, she was definitely out of her depth with this one. By opening half an hour early, I have a hunch she thought she could have the camera crew in and out before the likes of Shouting Barbara came along to complicate matters, but she vastly underestimated the process. The crew was still there when I went at lunch time to start the school lifts, by which time Barbara had been in for an extended nosy-parking visit, which had the sound recordist ripping off his headphones and muttering about going up to Casualty. Our *Appeal* goes out this Sunday night.

* * *

I simply want Lucy to tell me how to stop ruining my life by being a perfectionist, but she has started on all this other stuff about how different things are right for different people. I find it hard to disagree openly with her, as she is only trying to help me, but I honestly feel it is a cop-out when people say this about what is and isn't right. I mean, I know different *clothes* suit different people, but morality is a little more substantial than a matter of cut or colour.

* * *

Everyone at the shop is still talking about our visit from the television crew. Even the builders. They were filmed, too. The new drop-in centre in progress was filmed; the shop was filmed; and, apparently, who else but Prentiss Prine was then filmed yesterday, listening (and they say the camera never lies) to a client in her own home. In fact, it wasn't a real client, as they were considered too vulnerable to be outed on local television, it was actually one of our other Angels *posing* as a client. Seemingly, Mrs Nilsson was delighted with the lengths to which the camera crew went to get everything just right. We can't wait to see ourselves on Sunday.

* * *

I have made an appointment with the optician! (How on Earth will I dare to show up with my faceful of optical wreckage, though?)

* * *

Two updates regarding Woods's situation: (1) His big trauma was not that he got knocked down by a speeding car. In fact, he had a heart attack that made him fall out towards the road, but only his hand was run over. (2) He isn't going to die. At least, not yet. It is true that he wasn't expected to live, and Wendy was even asked if he was a card-carrying participant of the organ-donor scheme, but then he started to rally unexpectedly and now he's going to have a bit of a rest before they give him a triple by-pass operation.

One update regarding my situation: he has moved back home. He hasn't actually said anything, and I certainly haven't, but ever since Woods's accident, when he phoned me (and *didn't* seemingly phone Prentiss, which has apparently quite ticked her off), he has been behaving as if he still lives with us. Granted, he has been spending every free hour at Woods's bedside, and we do live nearer than Prentiss to the hospital, but when he does come home, this is where he comes home to, despite the mess and the disorder and the absence of healing massages.

Today, at the hospital, I also bumped into Marilyn, who had been visiting Philomena, the t'ai chi teacher, who is still bed-ridden. However, apparently Philomena's accident has given her a whole new career path: while in traction, Philomena felt she still needed to do her daily t'ai chi, so she has adapted the moves to suit someone who can only lie down or perhaps sit. This, in turn, gave her the idea that there is a whole community of elderly people out there in care homes who could do the same sitting-down t'ai chi movements, and she has been spending millions of ten and twenty pence pieces on the wheelie payphone on her ward, phoning round and making arrangements, with enormous success. Some people are so inventive!

* * *

Deidre Duffy, the school mummy whom I alleged was an alcoholic, came into the shop today with a people-carrier full of second-hand baby and toddler stuff. She had seen us on the telly last night and felt moved to act. Lorna, Kathleen, Margaret and I had also seen ourselves on the telly last night and felt moved to get facelifts, haircuts and posture lessons double quick, with suicide as a handier second option. We *hated* ourselves. And this was without our glasses, as we had been too vain to be seen on telly wearing them. (What's that about? Anybody who wants to can see us in our glasses in the shop any day of the week.) Through the miracle of television, we were able to see Shouting Barbara without hearing her, as she rocked her pram beside the counter in a background shot with a Mrs Nilsson voice-over (a good choice – Mrs Nilsson has a beautiful voice); there were shots of Kathleen ironing and Lorna and Margaret serving Seamus Kelly at the till (a real family album) and me in a hard hat carrying a tray of mugs to the builders. I had turned away from the clip of Prentiss doing her Listening Angel bit, but Kathleen and Lorna were able to tell me that after I had gone, they had discovered that the crew hadn't taken to her and had called her 'the big f***ing Yank line-dancer', and that the crew had even used a jokey line-dancing reference on the broadcast during the bit when I'd looked away and had shown a close-up of Prentiss's big boots!

When Deidre Duffy came in, she did that thing of talking far too much, and with unwarranted enthusiasm. It was a local television appeal, for goodness' sake, it wasn't *Art*. Once again, I could smell the drink fumes, and I struggled with the juxtaposition of these and the tangle of keys in her hand. I do not know what to do in situations like this. If I was heroic, wouldn't I seize the keys and refuse to allow her to drive her car until sober? Isn't it wrong to stand idly by? But it's not like she was falling off her feet or anything. She was just a lost-soul mother, trying to hide the fact that she had drink taken at eleven o'clock on a Monday morning, in her bally fleece and old trainers. I didn't even have the heart to tell her that it's our company policy not to sell on baby equipment, like her buggy and her cot, because someone higher up than us has decided that an accident might ensue through damaged goods, and we could be held liable. Which is fair enough, though at times a little embarrassing to administer. In Deidre's case, such was her effusive praise for our little venture, and such was her need to associate with it, I just took everything in and quietly explained to Margaret that, when Deidre had gone, I'd carry it all round the corner to the Salvation Army, who seem more confident about deciding which goods are fit for purpose and which aren't. I also asked Deidre to come and see us in our new drop-in centre, the opening of which is now imminent. Because it's new, it's easy to invite people to call in and we can pretend their visit is just out of interest and not because they are actually cracking up.

*　*　*

Lucy says I am obsessed with right ways and wrong ways. Well, she didn't exactly say that, but that was what she meant. I know what she's talking about, too, and sometimes it's so inappropriate I'm ashamed of myself. For example, sometimes a harrowed newsreader is reporting the latest details from some kind of humanitarian disaster and he or she will say something about less bodies being found today compared to yesterday and, instead of having a human feeling for the dead and the bereaved, my mind will fill with 'FEWER! It's FEWER bodies, not LESS bodies!' How obsessed with right and wrong is that?

Lucy didn't want to talk about the newsreaders, she wanted to talk about the food tins. She said it was *right* for the supermarket to put the tins with the labels facing out because it was their *raison d'être* to sell stuff, and to sell stuff you had to show the customers what you were actually selling. Therefore, she said, this showed that putting the tins facing forward was *right for them*, but that this was not the same as being *right full stop*. Did I feel the need to put all the tins in my shopping bag facing the front, Lucy wanted to know. I conceded that I did not. This, according to Lucy, substantiated her point. Could I recognise my tins of produce pretty well from the back instead of the front? Well, yes, I had to admit that I could. Lucy left it hanging, but she came dangerously close to saying there is no absolute right way to put tins in a cupboard, which is tantamount to saying that much of my adult life has been in vain!

Lucy did say that I have to stop beating myself up for failing to achieve some abstract notion of absolute right and start doing what's *right for me*. Whatever that means.

*

There is a 'situation' at the hospital with Woods's current girlfriend and Wendy. They pretend each other doesn't exist, which is straightforward enough as long as you are one of them. For the rest of us, it is very tricky acknowledging either one without offending the other.

*   *   *

Kathleen says Woods and his women are the whole talk of the men's ward. Apparently all the other inmates are envious because they think Woods got his heart attack from an excess of sex.

*

The builders have knocked a doorway through from our shop to the drop-in centre, so now we have an extra window on the world. It looks like they've nearly finished the job. Kathleen says she will miss them.

*   *   *

The political situation at Woods's bedside may be nearing

217

an end, since his girlfriend's black Vauxhall Corsa got scraped in the multi-storey car park. The perpetrator did it when the girlfriend was away from her car and then just drove off, so now the girlfriend spends her visit tapping her mule against the sole of her foot and checking her car-park ticket. Wendy doesn't care if someone scrapes her old Toyota hatchback. When she visits, she brings shepherd's pie in a thermal dish and reads Woods bits out of the newspaper. I think we can see whose tactics are winning.

(Just as I have taken so long to notice that Woods's charm is a virtue, I think he has taken so long to notice the same about Wendy's kindness towards him. But we've both noticed now.)

* * *

Kathleen is going to have a sun room (*not* a uPVC conservatory) added to her house. Does she really need another room to sit in by herself when she's not bringing Lucozade to her husband in hospital? I suspect it's at least partly because she has had such fun with our builders.

*

He has bought a Valentine card. It was in a paper bag inside his newspaper. The bag had slipped down an inch, and I could see the red upper part of the two humps that make the top of a love-heart. But is it for me . . . or her?

* * *

Lorna is going to move in with Kathleen! At least, for as long as Kathleen's husband is in hospital, which I sometimes suspect is going to be for ever, and perhaps Kathleen is of a similar impression. (And guess who's going to shift Lorna's stuff in his Renault Mégane? Seamus Kelly! He sort of seems to be becoming their surrogate son.) Kathleen says it's going to be great having the company and having someone there to make it worthwhile cooking a proper meal. Lorna intimated that she's looking forward to having someone to help her watch her *Dad's Army* videos, at which Kathleen's face visibly clouded with the first of what I hope will not be many doubts.

*

I have decided that it is *right for me* to lie to the optician when I attend my appointment and say that I have *lost* my old glasses.

* * *

Lucy wondered if I had religion. She thought perhaps this was where I had got the immovable sense of absolute right I have been using to truncheon myself into failure. I told her I did not, but that I did have role models like Gandhi and Jesus and Martin Luther King. I reminded her that Jesus had said there was only one way to enlightenment, and hadn't Gandhi taught that to have integrity and inner peace, you had to *think* and *say* and *do* all the same thing? Lucy said, 'Nice verk iff you can get it.' And then I told her

219

about the Holy Land and not having a religious experience and the smell of urine and the sofa on the Via Dolorosa, and she said, 'You see, lissen to yourself. You know already. One man's path to death and glory and, for the little children, it was just some place to play chase.'

No Valentine card. Not for me, anyway.

*   *   *

As an act of rebellion against my old demons, I have taken the labels off all the tins in the cupboard and spun each one round until I don't know where the front is. Then I put them back in the cupboard. Hurray, I am liberated!

*

We have had sausages and mash with custard for tea. It could have been worse. But guess what, he *laughed* about it. We hadn't seen him do that for a while.

(The children, being children, actually preferred their dinner served with custard.)

*

A team of men is coming to put up a shed in Eleanor and Terry's back garden tomorrow. Eleanor is really excited. It is actually more of a summer house than a shed – it has its own veranda and criss-crossed doll's-house windows. So now I don't know if the shed is for Terry or Eleanor to play in.

*

(The two red love-heart humps were not red love-heart humps. They were the tops of two red balloons on the get-well card he had finally got round to buying for Woods. People must have wondered why I was so inexplicably smiley at visiting today. I even bought the children a bag of disgusting gummy sweets at the hospital shop. Well, why not, now that I can afford to? Now that I'm getting new glasses, I'll be able to take them back to their pass-remarkable dentist.)

* * *

Prentiss Prine has resigned her listening job and is leaving Ivy Cottage to return to the States. It came to us on the Angels' grapevine at the shop. She is intending to bring the healing power of reiki to her own troubled family, then set up a practice to the benefit of her corner of the USA. She is not intending to bring Earl back with her and has made it known that he is house-trained and now needs a house.

* * *

We have had the vasectomy conversation. He is going to go ahead with the new National Health date. At last, I am fully glad. We have the three assorted children we have, and they are wonderful, and now there is the Angels' project and the market-stall job, and it is *right for us* to enjoy what we have and not risk messing it all up with an ill-conceived heartbreak.

*

221

(He never actually had sex with Prentiss. At least, that is what he says, and I believe him. Not because he's so honest (we know he isn't) but because it sounds just like Prentiss to say what he says she said about sexual intimacy, which I can't even be bothered to relate: it's that stupid.)

* * *

I took Lucy round the Notes for the Next Time and asked her if I should burn them. She took them from me and looked at them slowly. Then she said, 'Let's not throw the baby out vith the vater from the bath.' Lucy, who it turns out has produced several self-help books, is going to show them to her publisher!

*

The Angels are having a promotional stand and a flag day in the high-street mall next week, and Margaret has asked Lorna, Kathleen and me to help staff it. I said I would be willing to put in the hours, happy to wear the T-shirt but refused to put on the baseball cap. Margaret looked surprised but said that was all right.

*

It was in the *Oldie* magazine that Dr Susan McPeake is not a real doctor! Jeffrey Devine should be ashamed. And to think that he used to present *Newstalk*!

*

What with everything that's been going on, I had

completely overlooked the possibility of e-mail, and, of course, one such has been lying unopened in my computer since December when Rachel returned from the world-famous German markets. Rachel is no longer a child-minder, she says. Her boyfriend has set her up in business as a mobile nail technician. As he is a builder, you might think this is some kind of peripatetic supplier of construction-industry sundries, but in fact it just means Rachel wears a white tunic and lots of make-up and files and paints women's fingernails. Rachel says the surest way of me getting back together with *him* is if she were to badmouth him to me because she's done this for friends in the past, in sincerity, and the couples have always got back together and then hated her, but she says she wouldn't mind us hating her so much because she doesn't even see us any more. Rachel also suggested, if that didn't work, then maybe the break-up would be the start of something new for me, and perhaps I would meet someone better. She reminded me, 'What's this you used to say, "Greet the unseen with a smile"?' It was 'with a cheer', actually. She went on to ask me whether I had said 'Shit' or 'Fuck' when I had seen them coming out of Mumbles hand in hand, and remarked that if all else failed, at least I had the perfect excuse for playing my Edith Piaf records at full volume. And I thought, Rachel, all that is so last year, because the truth is, I hadn't done any of those things. At that moment, I realised that I, the great stuck one, had possibly begun to move.

* * *

I saw Jill out roller blading today. She looked cool in skater-pose, but I do not wish to swap my life for hers. I am not perfect – I still blink a bit too much, think a bit too much, probably – but just for now I don't want to be.

Just for now, I am enough.

Epilogue

Things were quiet in the market today, so after Marilyn had taken her lunch-time toilet break, she said I could go, and I dropped into the drop-in centre for an hour. The man with two hats was there, as usual, drinking tea, and Deidre Duffy passed me on her way into the group room, where I know she goes twice a week, as do I. As I was talking to Seamus Kelly, who is with us on an adult gap-year, it came up that between the centre, the shop, Marilyn's stall and the school runs, I still have a 'window' between twelve thirty and two p.m. every weekday that I can call my own.

'You could have an affair,' Seamus ventured, knowing that he and I have already discussed and dismissed this possibility, mainly on the basis of my disagreeable teeth.

'Or write a novel with very short chapters,' I suggested, also not for the first time.

'Or,' replied Seamus, who really is very handsome, 'what's to stop you from doing both?'

Acknowledgements

Thanks go to Daragh Carville and Glenn Patterson at Queen's University, Belfast; Faith O'Grady at the Lisa Richards Agency; Breda Purdue, Ciara Considine, Ciara Doorley and Peter McNulty at Hodder Headline Ireland; Hazel Orme; all the Messies out there in cyberspace; and, of course, and especially, to Robin and Myra, Niall, Keir, Clem and Nye.